Ella Mae

A NOVEL

MYRTLE MCDANIEL

WinePressPublishing
Great Books, Defined.

To all of my family and everyone who knew and
loved Ella Mae—or someone like her

Contents

Preface

ELLA MAE IS the story of an ordinary woman and the struggles and circumstances that shaped her life as a wife and mother. She lived in an era when our country was largely agricultural, when living on a farm made folks both dependent and independent. They were dependent upon large landowners who needed the help of farmers to grow and harvest their crops. They were independent because they could provide for themselves no matter where they lived. It was a time of making do and trusting God to bless those who trusted in Him.

This story will bring back many memories of the "good old days" that are quickly disappearing in our fast-paced, technological age. Some will entertain, and some will cause us to examine what is important and of lasting value to us and our children.

Ella Mae

The story of Ella Mae is partly fiction, but it is true to the times and the way things were in those days. She, and others like her, left a legacy of endurance and faith to her family and all who knew her. It would do us and our country well to learn from her and imitate her character.

CHAPTER 1

Moving Day

ELLA MAE STOOD in the lane and watched the truck carrying all their belongings until it was out of sight. It not only held their belongings, but also those precious to her. Her husband, Avery, and their sons Riley and Garvin had chosen to go with the truck to help unload the furniture when the truck arrived at its destination.

A feeling of desolation, unlike anything she ever had experienced, swept over her heart. She had thought she was prepared to leave Grassy Creek and all she had ever known, to follow Avery to a completely new and different place. But she was wrong. She knew nothing about Maryland, except that it seemed very far away. She was not ready.

It was not the moving she minded. In the years she had been married to Avery, they had moved several times. As their family continued to grow, the need for more space kept increasing. Each move was supposed to be an improvement, either in circumstances or the size of the house. But the moves had always been within visiting distance of family and friends. There never had been a need for long good-byes or the shedding of tears—until now.

Mae looked around at the home they had created there in the hills. When Avery bought the land and, with the help of a neighbor, built their very own house, Mae had expected this to be the last move. She also had expected Mary Lou to be her last child. But seven years later, after Foster had left home to go into business and Faye had entered nurses training, Baby Jo Angeline was born. This increased the number of Mae's children to eight; plus Granny, Mae's mother, who lived with them.

Mae's mother was a midwife, so it had seemed natural that she came to help Mae when it was time for her first child to be born. Avery and Mae's first home was a one-room cabin, which seemed to work fine for the two of them. But the arrival of the new baby made it necessary to have larger living quarters, especially after it became evident that Granny intended to stay for some time. She never left.

Life was hard. Coming out of the Great Depression, there was little or no money to be had. Mae had always felt they were blessed. They had plenty to eat, and with a little horse trading on the side, Avery was able to provide for his family.

Their home was a place where people loved to congregate. There was always laughter and a story to tell. A favorite family tale was how Mae's mother got her name. No one in that entire area ever heard her called anything but Granny. It seemed that when the children were playing one day, Foster called her "Granny" instead of the usual "Grandma" as he had been taught. After Mae heard him repeatedly call her "Granny," she asked him why he kept saying that, especially since he knew better.

"I like the way it sounds. It's more friendly," Foster answered.

Granny overheard this conversation, and since it was said with love and not disrespect, "Granny" became her name from then on.

Mae was an excellent cook. They grew their own vegetables and raised their own meat. They had cows and chickens for milk and butter and eggs. No one ever left their house hungry. Hardly a Sunday passed that someone did not come home with them from church for a good meal and pleasant fellowship.

The first time the strangers from the north visited Grassy Creek, Mae had been afraid. These were men who owned big farms in Maryland and Pennsylvania and were looking for cheap labor to help them make their farms productive. They especially were interested in families that had sons big enough to help with the work. These visits marked the beginning of a great exodus of people from the mountains, where there was little or no industry, to the northern states, where they could find work and better opportunities for their children. Seeing their closest neighbors and her dear friends pack up and leave had almost broken Mae's heart.

Mae had sensed that one day Avery would approach her with the desire to look beyond the hills for "the land of milk and honey." Well, that day had come, and they were joining the stream of those leaving for the "Promised Land." She was skeptical about the promises. She was not ready!

There was a memory everywhere Mae looked. From the new chicken house Avery had built, to the apple trees they had planted, to the garden with the raspberry patch in the center, to the springhouse (where the food was kept cold), to the big bean tree that shaded her kitchen. She stored the memories away to take with her for the times when she might need a touch of home. This would always be home, no matter how far away they moved.

Mae returned to the house and walked through the rooms one last time. It was getting late, and the neighbors who had offered hospitality for Mae and the children's last night would be coming for her soon. Her children, Eileen, Ben, Mary Lou, and Jo, already were at the neighbors.

Mae paused by the window to pray for the right attitude and strength to be the kind of wife and mother Jesus wanted her to be. She recalled the preacher's sermon on Sunday. It had seemed to be directed to her need. In her mind, she heard again Paul's words to the church in Philippi: "Forgetting those things which are behind, and reaching forth to those things which are before, I press toward the mark for the prize of the high calling of God in Christ Jesus." She whispered, "Dear Lord, teach me how to follow and not look back. Help me to live for each day, to be the kind of wife and mother that will be pleasing to You."

CHAPTER 2

Northward Bound

ELLA MAE LAID Baby Jo across the pillow on her lap and covered her with a soft blanket. Granny slid into the car, settled down beside Mae, and then closed the door. She pulled half of the pillow across her lap, giving her daughter a little more room. Ben, Eileen, and Mary Lou climbed into the back seat among boxes containing things for the baby and food for lunch. It was going to be a long, crowded trip from Grassy Creek, North Carolina, to Maryland, but they were on their way at last.

Five thirty in the morning was still the deep dark just before dawn that was not quite the end of night and not yet the beginning of the new day. Uncle Carl pressed the starter, and the car roared to life. With a final wave to the kind neighbors who had provided them shelter for the night, their journey out of the hills began.

"Well, Mae, are you sure you have everything? Are you ready to go?" Uncle Carl watched her out of the corner of his eye as he guided the car down the lane and onto the highway. While he was delighted to have his brother and his family move closer to him, he understood this was not an easy transition for Mae. He was not positive his own wife would take such a move so well.

"I guess I'm as ready as I'll ever be," Mae pressed her lips together and made herself busy adjusting the position of the baby. She really wanted to say, "No, I'm not ready, and I won't be ready tomorrow or the next day or the next." But of course, she didn't. In reality, she wanted to put her head down and cry her heart out, but she stared straight ahead, hoping to catch a glimpse of the last of the familiar hillsides. Unfortunately, it was too dark to see beyond the small sphere of the headlights' beams.

Carl drove steadily. He only stopped for gas, timing these stops so that his passengers had a chance to relieve themselves and stretch their legs. Conversation was patchy and mostly between Granny and Carl. Around noon, they stopped at a combination gas station and general store. Three or four picnic tables were located to one side of the building, and even though the air was cold, everyone was glad for the chance to move around. Granny and Eileen unpacked lunch while Mae took care of Baby Jo's needs. Carl treated the adults to cups of hot coffee and Ben and Mary Lou to some milk.

As tired as they were of being cramped together all morning, it felt good to get back into the warm car and get moving again. They passed through several towns and a few cities. Eileen got excited every time she recognized the name of a place like Roanoke, the Shenandoah Valley, or Washington, DC. At some other time these places would be interesting to see, but what they looked forward to now was reaching Uncle Claude and Aunt Laura's house, where they could get a good, warm meal and go to bed.

Mae thought about the rest of her family, who were in the truck somewhere on the road ahead. Then she thought about Avery's cousin, the driver of the truck, who had agreed to move them almost 650 miles from their home in North Carolina to a farm in Maryland, where there was work and a good living to be made—or so the talk had been that culminated in this trip.

Carl continued to make good time, but it seemed like many hours before they pulled into the driveway of a fairly large, two-story, stone house. It was late afternoon when Avery's sister, Aunt Laura, came to meet them and took the baby from Granny's lap. She hurried into the warm kitchen before the cold air had a chance to ruffle the baby's blanket.

"Hello, younguns, come on in! I know you are tired to death. Mae, how are you? About wore out, I can tell. Well, supper will be ready just as soon as Claude gets finished with the milking. Come right in and make yourselves at home."

Carl helped the tired women with their bags and bundles. After greeting Laura and assuring Mae he would return in the morning to take her to her new home, he backed out of the driveway and went toward his own home. Although invited to stay for supper, Carl said he didn't want to miss the warm welcome and good dinner that would be waiting for him.

Uncle Claude finished his day's work and entered the back door just as Avery and a weary Riley and Garvin were being dropped off in front of the house. The cousin who had brought their furniture from Grassy Creek was staying at a nearby boarding house.

Aunt Laura had supper on the table by the time greetings were over and hands and faces were washed. When everyone was seated at the long table, hands were joined and heads bowed. Uncle Claude thanked the Lord for their safe arrival and for providing them with this food. He also remembered to be thankful for Aunt Laura's work in preparing such an abundant table.

Steaming platters of hot biscuits, fried ham, and red-eye gravy, along with bowls heaped with mashed potatoes swimming in butter, green beans from Laura's well-stocked cellar, and spicy applesauce were passed around the table. Jelly, apple butter, and fresh-churned butter were there for the biscuits. Hot coffee for the adults and large glasses of fresh milk were provided for the children. Plates were emptied and refilled until everyone was satisfied.

After supper, Mae noticed the heads of Ben and Mary Lou drooping over their plates. Eileen helped Aunt Laura take them upstairs and tuck them into their beds. They did not even notice the noise of voices as the adults talked about the happenings of the day; they were sound asleep as soon as their heads touched the pillows. Although she was as tired as the children, Eileen returned downstairs to help clean up the kitchen. The men pushed their chairs back from the table and retired to the living room, where a nice fire was blazing in the fireplace.

Ordinarily, the grownups would continue to sit and talk until the wee hours. There was a lot of family news to catch up on. But since they had already experienced a hard day of travel and were looking ahead to an equally busy day of putting the new home in order, everyone soon went to bed.

Uncle Claude got up every morning at four o'clock to begin milking. It was decided that would be a good time for everyone else to get up and prepare for their day. Only Ben, Mary Lou, and Granny were allowed to sleep, as they were not going to the new house just yet.

CHAPTER 3

A New Home

AVERY TOOK RILEY and Garvin to the barn with Claude while the women put breakfast on the table. This was a much larger farm than the one to which they were going, but he wanted them to observe the workings of the dairy. Surely there would be something they could learn and put to use in one way or another.

Claude proudly explained all that he was doing and why, without pausing in his work. He had been one of the earliest to take part in the great migration of farm workers from the South, to what proved for so many to be the "land of milk and honey." It had been that for Claude, and he realized and acknowledged his good fortune.

11

After the milking was finished, Claude paused outside the back door and let the boys go into breakfast. "Avery, you've got a chance to make a good life for yourself and your family, and I know you will work hard. Just be careful, and keep your eyes and ears open."

"What are you trying to tell me, Claude?"

"Just what I said: be careful. It's a good farm you are going to, or it could be. Word has it that the man you're going to work for is tight with his money and not above taking advantage of the men who work for him. That's all I'm saying."

By the time everyone finished a hearty breakfast of oatmeal, sausage, scrambled eggs, milk gravy over hot biscuits, and strong black coffee, Carl was pulling into the driveway. Laura insisted they should go and not wait to clear the table. So without further ado, Avery and Mae climbed in beside Carl, and Eileen, Riley, and Garvin crowded into the back seat. Eileen took charge of Baby Jo, who was still nursing, making it necessary to take her along. No one thought to look back to see the frightened faces of Mary Lou and Ben pushed against the upstairs window. Carl eased the car onto the highway and headed for Maryville and the house that was waiting for its new occupants.

The rolling hills of that ten-mile drive were very pleasant to the transplanted family away from their own familiar home. The pretty houses they passed, the neat barns with cows in the meadows, seemed to fulfill the promises that had lured them to leave North Carolina.

As they passed a white barn needing a fresh coat of paint that was located very close to the highway, Carl slowed down. Avery spoke to his family, "Well, boys, there is the place where we'll be working in a couple of days."

Everyone looked with interest. Mae could see that they couldn't help comparing the rundown appearance of this barn with the one they had just left. However, nothing was said.

They soon got a glimpse of a large house set on the hillside behind the barn, nestled in a group of maple trees. Mae wondered, *Is this where we will live?*

Carl drove on until they were almost out of sight of the barn and then pulled off the road and stopped in front of a long building that looked like it was ready to fall down.

Why is he stopping here? Mae could see that the main part of the structure was part of a log cabin of an undetermined age that had been added onto in some long ago time. The entire building was a soft, weather-beaten gray that comes from long exposure to the elements. It was evident it had never known a coat of paint. The one redeeming feature was a long porch, which seemed to have been added recently. Perhaps that was what kept the whole building from collapsing to the ground.

It was not until Avery got out of the car and gave Riley a key to open the front door that Mae realized this was their new home. She was not sure what she had expected but certainly not this dilapidated, ancient... She was so shocked she could not even think of a word to describe what she was seeing. Without thinking, a remembrance of the little white house in North Carolina imposed itself on her mind.

"Well, come on, Mae," Avery held the car door open and extended his hand to assist her from the car. "I know it's not pretty, but it's not so bad once you see the inside and get your things placed around. It's not like it will be forever."

Mae moved like one in a stupor. She looked at Riley and Garvin, neither of whom would meet her gaze. They did not say a word, but she could tell they knew what was going through her mind.

Garvin carefully helped Eileen descend from the car without waking the baby. She held the little one close to make sure she stayed warm. She obviously was looking for something to do so that she did not have to look at her mother and see the disappointment on her face.

Mae tried to remember what Avery had told them about the house when he was trying to persuade her to make this move. All she could recall was the talk of electricity and how they would all get ahead in life by taking this opportunity.

Avery commented about how he was glad he had made sure both the living room stove and the old, black kitchen range had been set up the day before. Kindling had been arranged so that all Riley had to do was strike a match and a fire was quickly blazing. As soon as a little wood was added to this small blaze, they had heat enough to knock the chill from the air.

Mae realized the whole tenor of the years ahead depended on her reaction to this place that was to be her home for at least the next two years. She darted a quick glance at Avery and could see that he was holding his breath to gauge her acceptance or rejection of this place to which he had enticed her. He obviously realized it was far below what she had expected. Mae wondered if he wished he had not been so quick to accept the offer Mr. Jennings had made.

Mae was positive he had considered the potential of the good farmland that was all around them. Perhaps he had not given enough thought to the needs of his wife and family. She tried to remember that their life was more than a house. All she did remember was that she must not cry.

Mae walked across the porch and laid her hand on Avery's arm. "Well, Avery, are you going to carry me across the threshold, or must I just walk in? We really need to get the baby in out of the cold." She dared not say more, or the tears would flow. She suddenly believed their love was on trial. *"Please, Lord, guide my steps and my mouth. Stay close."*

Avery opened the door and stooped to pick her up. Even though she blocked his efforts, she did not stop him from dropping a quick kiss on her cold cheek before he helped her into the house. The children, who did not often see such open demonstrations of affection between their parents, seemed to let out their breath in a collective sigh of relief. Mae hoped they knew she was going to be OK and that they would make it, even in this old house, because they could count on their mother to make it a home.

"Bravo, Avery!" called Uncle Carl. "You've still got it! Whatever '*it*' is. Now, I've got to get going, but I'll be back in time to pick you up for supper."

Avery grinned, shook Carl's hand, and watched as he backed across the yard and onto the highway.

Now it was time to get to work. With the strength that came from the One who heard her silent prayer, Mae stepped into the living room and looked around. Their sparse furniture was stacked here and there with only enough room for a path to the rest of the house. She was pleased with the size of the living room.

Avery lost no time in showing her the adjoining room, which was to be their bedroom. Privacy, which they had not enjoyed since the birth of their firstborn son, would be a real pleasure. They never had lived in a house big enough to house all of their children in rooms of their own before.

She noticed with a smile how Avery flipped on the lights in each room, even though it was broad daylight.

Much of his persuasive talk about this move had been about the marvels of electricity. Now, he wanted her to notice it. She tried not to think about the soft glow of their Aladdin lamp as they gathered in the living room in Grassy Creek.

Garvin pulled a chair up close to the big stove for Eileen and the baby. By this time, it was beginning to throw off heat. He proceeded to add a sizable chunk of wood to the flames and went to check on the fire in the kitchen.

Riley had already taken care of this chore. The old, black range was doing its duty, and it, too, was providing some heat to the room. He rummaged around in the boxes marked "Kitchen" until he found the two cast iron kettles. He then proceeded out the back door to the hand pump on the stoop. By the time he had filled the kettles and placed them on the stove to heat, Avery was bringing Mae into the kitchen.

It was easy to see this section was the part that had been added onto the original building. Mae was glad to see the kitchen was large enough to accommodate their long table. With their bench that went along one side and the chairs they had brought, currently laden with boxes containing their cooking and food supplies, along the other, there was space to comfortably seat all eight of them. And they easily could make room for more seats whenever that was needed.

17

Mae looked over the rough cupboards that covered the wall next to the living room and on either side of a double window on the outside wall. Shelves on one side of the stove would be handy for pots and pans. Cupboards under the windows seemed a good place to store canned goods.

Satisfied that the kitchen was able to supply their need for plenty of elbowroom, Mae followed Avery back into the living room. A door in one corner opened to narrow stairs leading upwards to a long hallway ending in a large room with space for all three boys. It even could hold four beds, if necessary. A room directly over the living room would do nicely for Eileen and Mary Lou. Another, smaller room over the kitchen had a ceiling that tapered down on each side with low windows made to provide good ventilation in the summer. A metal grate located in the floor directly over the cook stove would help convey warmth during the winter. Mae thought the privacy would please Granny, but there was a little worry about her ability to climb the narrow stairs.

Mae was pleased to see that Mr. Jennings had been thoughtful enough to have his grandson paint the upstairs rooms, except for the one that was to be Granny's. They must put Riley and Garvin to painting that one as soon as possible. Mr. Jennings had left about a half gallon of paint in the room, and it would be enough to do the walls. It was a new kind of paint called Kal-O-Mine that came in powder form. When mixed with water to the consistency one wanted, it covered the surface very nicely, dried quickly, and left very little odor. That was just what they needed. Mae wanted the room ready before her mother saw it.

Mae and Avery returned to the warmth of the downstairs. Baby Jo was wide awake and beginning to fuss. Avery pulled a rocking chair into their bedroom for Mae. While she prepared to nurse the hungry baby, he gently covered them both with one of their patchwork quilts. He lightly patted Mae's arm, then left to give the boys a hand in putting their beds together.

Mae was glad for the rest and the few moments alone. She struggled to get herself under control, knowing she must banish the visions of the little house in North Carolina that kept coming between thoughts of what she had left behind and what she was seeing. Wearily, she gathered the quilt more closely around her and snuggled the baby close to her breast. She wanted to cry, but knew she ought not. The children were watching her closely. The way she reacted to the changes in their surroundings would set the way they would respond to life in this house. It was up to her to encourage Avery and establish the pattern for their way of life in the days ahead. How she was to do that was unclear for the moment, but she realized that God already knew what was ahead and was aware of the way her steps should go. After all, what was coming into a strange land where everything was different, compared to His coming from glory to a place that certainly was a marked contrast to His heavenly home? He not only had given up all that was His due, but also He had done it gladly, out of a heart of love for mankind, even for her. Mae began praying for patience and wisdom.

While Mae was spending time caring for the baby, Eileen hurried to the kitchen. Without asking or arguing, she took charge of getting things organized. Riley did her bidding and soon had the cardboard boxes on the table emptied and stacked beside the stove. Later they would cut them apart to use for starting the fires in the two stoves.

Eileen poured hot water into the dishpan and handed the kettle to Riley to refill. Grabbing a bar of yellow soap, she vigorously started scrubbing the cupboard shelves. While she was getting the cupboards ready, Riley started unpacking the dishes. By the time Eileen was finished with the shelves, more hot water was ready, enough to fill two dishpans—one for washing and one for rinsing.

With an assembly line approach, the clean dishes soon were lined up on the shelves wherever Riley could find room. No doubt they would be rearranged when everything was unpacked, but for now, they easily could see what was ready to be used.

Riley rummaged through more boxes until he located the coffee pot and another box marked "Food," where he found a tin of coffee. He pumped a bucket of fresh water, and soon the odor of good, strong coffee filled the air.

Meanwhile, Avery and Garvin carried Granny's boxes and her furniture up the stairs and into her room. Plans were made to begin painting the room before anything was arranged. Granny would want the final say as to where her possessions belonged anyway. Besides her rocking chair, there was an oak washstand; her bed; a large, square, metal-covered trunk; and a smaller trunk with a domed top covered with red and blue strips of metal and nail-studded designs on the sides. When the last trip was made up the narrow, winding stairs, the two men were ready for a break.

Mae changed and rocked Baby Jo until she was sound asleep. Avery opened the door to see how everything was going. Noting how tired he seemed, Mae motioned for him to remove the quilt from around her and the baby. Quietly, she stood and bade him to sit in the vacated chair. He looked surprised when she handed him the sleeping baby.

Like Mae before him, Avery looked glad for a little respite from the heavy work of the morning. He held the baby close to his chest. It was the first time since they began loading their furniture onto the truck in North Carolina that he had actually taken time to really look at her, let alone hold her.

Avery had almost nodded off when Eileen and Riley issued the call to dinner. Mae reclaimed the baby and laid her in the middle of the bed, surrounding her with pillows. These would serve as a barrier in case she rolled over. Mae and Avery hastened to follow the welcoming scent of coffee to the kitchen.

The remaining boxes had been removed from the table and the lunch Aunt Laura had prepared for them opened. It was truly a grateful prayer that was offered from the hearts of the hungry family—not only for the food but also for the chance to take time to talk a minute.

It was decided that Riley and Garvin should paint Granny's room so that it would dry before they assembled her bed. Eileen and Mae would continue putting the kitchen in order while Avery followed through on his arrangements to go to town with Mr. Jennings in order to take care of the business connected with moving.

The first stop Avery made was at the high school. He introduced himself to the principal and left the school records, transferring Riley and Garvin from North Carolina to Maryland. A stop at the post office to change their address, another at the bank to open an account, and quick stops at a few places of business, where Mr. Jenkins introduced him, made it past time to go home.

Avery returned just a few minutes before Carl came to take them back to Claude and Laura's house for the night. Everyone was glad to stop their work for the day and head for the good supper Aunt Laura would have waiting for them.

Mae was surprised at the looks of relief on the faces of Ben and Mary Lou when they first arrived. Throughout the evening, Ben stayed glued to her side and Mary Lou snuggled against Eileen. Granny later told Mae that the children had not left the window all afternoon. Aunt Laura had turned their care over to Granny. Other than seeing that they came to the table for lunch, she had been too busy to try to entertain them.

Mae knew Granny was not one to play games. Nor did she get down on the floor, as Eileen would have done, to play with the children. She could entertain grownups all day long, but she did not connect too well with young children. Her attempts to persuade Ben and Mary Lou to take a nap never had been successful. The children seemed to be afraid of Granny, but Mae was not sure why.

As Mae watched her children, she realized that they must have felt like everyone who cared about them was gone and they were in a house that seemed dark and gloomy. The later the day became, the more their fears must have increased. Mae was glad that everyone was together again and her children's world had righted itself.

Tired as the adults were, they stayed up long enough to visit a little while. Avery and Mae exchanged all the family news with their hosts. And they made sure that Claude and Laura knew how much their hospitality was appreciated.

Carl suggested that Granny come to their house for a few days to give Mae and Eileen time to get the house organized. He would bring her home the following Saturday. Everyone seemed to think this was a good idea, especially Mae. This would give her time to make sure Granny's room was presentable before she came. After a muttered grumble or two about being in the way, Granny agreed.

Uncle Claude made their nighttime prayer very short, as he knew their tired bodies were longing for the feather beds that were waiting for them.

Ben and Mary Lou were much relieved the next morning to find they would not be left alone again. They eagerly climbed into the crowded car that took them to the house that was to be home for them. They did not pay much attention to the appearance of the house. The important thing was that they were all together. No one was left behind.

They were all glad to see that the stoves were still warm when they entered the house. Avery added a little wood to the glowing embers, and a good fire quickly was giving off heat to the chilly rooms. They were soon able to take off their coats and get to work.

"Now, children," Avery gave instructions, "you all must do your best to get everything done that is necessary today. Tomorrow, I must begin work, and you will begin school, so don't waste any time. Four o'clock in the morning will come early. I must meet with Mr. Jenkins today and go over every detail of our contract to be certain all is in order. Then I have to go down to the barn and check with his grandson to see that everything is ready for me to take over. I want to look over the equipment and make sure I understand the work in the dairy and about the feeding schedule, etc. I doubt if I will be home until suppertime."

After Avery left, Mae went to tend to the baby and get her settled for the morning. The rest of the family proceeded up the stairs and set to work.

After showing Ben and Mary Lou all the rooms and explaining who would be in each one, Eileen took Mary Lou to the room they would share. The first thing they had to do was locate and unpack clean sheets to make the beds. Adding warm quilts and pillows put the finishing touches on that job.

"You can look in the top drawer of the dresser and choose a pretty doily for the top," Eileen told Mary Lou.

Mary Lou promptly chose a scarf that was long enough to cover the entire top of the dresser. It had been embroidered with bright yellow flowers. She carefully placed her brush and comb beside those of her big sister; then she stood back to admire her work.

Mary Lou stood by the bed without moving for several minutes. Eileen could see that something was troubling the child. She kept twisting one hand inside the other. She waited for Mary Lou to speak.

"Do we have to go back to that other house? I don't like it there," Mary Lou finally said.

Eileen looked down at the forlorn face of her little sister. "No, dear, we won't be going back there. But don't you think it was nice of Aunt Laura to take care of us until we could come to this house?"

"Yes, but we didn't know them, and the house was scary. I missed Mama and you all. Ben did too."

Eileen sat down on the bed and pulled Mary Lou onto her lap, reassuring her that this would be home. She then reminded her that they needed to be thankful for Aunt Laura and Uncle Claude. "She was a good cook, wasn't she? I noticed that you ate all your dinner."

"Yes, but Mama's better!"

It was sometime later that Eileen learned that Ben had stated similar worries to Garvin.

Satisfied, and with Mary Lou's concerns settled, they went across the hall to watch Riley put the finishing touches on the painting of Granny's room. He was almost finished and gave Mary Lou a brush and showed her how to look for spots he had missed. It was obvious she felt very important to be included in the work of getting settled. She was busily going around the room inspecting the paint when the noise of children shouting caused her to run to the boys' room.

Ben and Garvin were looking out the window, watching a small group of children in a fenced yard across the meadow from their house.

"That's the school where you will be going in the morning," Garvin explained. "It must be recess time. It looks like the children are playing tag."

At the sound of a bell, the children ran to a small building and lined up at the door. They watched as someone opened the door from the inside and the children marched in.

"At least it's close enough for you to walk, and you can come home for lunch. We have to ride the bus, and Mother will have to pack our lunches."

"Before that, we must finish making these beds and then get your clothes laid out for the morning. I'm sure your shirts will need ironing. Mother will want you to look your best at the new school," Eileen said, calling them back to their duties.

Eileen descended the stairs to find her mother down on her hands and knees going along the baseboard in the living room with a feather in her hand. She was dipping the feather into a can of kerosene and dragging the feather along the top of the baseboard.

"Mother, what in the world are you doing?"

"I'm making sure that no bed bugs or spiders or other critters are going to get in our beds. We don't know who has lived here and how nasty or clean they were. This is just a precaution, and it is one that works."

Eileen laughed and offered to relieve her mother of the task, but Mae was almost finished. She already had been around the bedroom and kitchen baseboards. The entire house smelled of kerosene, but a blast of cold air from the door soon would take care of that.

The two women decided to prepare their first supper a little early. They peeled potatoes, opened a can of pork tenderloin, and chopped a small head of cabbage Laura had sent. Mae made biscuits while Eileen set the table. They decided to use a lace tablecloth, as this was a special time. Tomorrow would mark a new beginning for all of them.

CHAPTER 4

School Days

*A*VERY SAID AN especially tender prayer at breakfast, asking God to watch over the children as they attended school.

Once they were finished eating, he said, "Children, you will be on display today. Everyone will be watching you because you are strangers to them. Be careful of your manners, and don't do or say anything that would be an embarrassment to anyone in our family. Now hurry and get dressed. You don't want to be late the first day."

All the family gathered by the front window to watch Riley and Garvin get on the bus that would carry them to their high school. As soon as the bus was gone, Mae made sure Mary Lou and Ben were ready to walk across the meadow to the small schoolhouse they had seen from the window. Avery would have walked with them, but he said he thought Ben would like it better if Mary Lou and he went by themselves. After all, he was in sixth grade.

The teacher, a Catholic nun, greeted Ben and Mary Lou at the door and introduced herself as Sister Anne.

Both of the children stared at Sister Anne, simply out of curiosity, because they never had seen anyone dressed in a habit or heard anyone called "Sister" before. In fact, they never had heard of or seen a Catholic before at all.

Sister Anne mistook their frank appraisal for rudeness, and it made her a little angry.

After Ben handed her Mary Lou's and his records from North Carolina, Sister Anne took them to the front of the room and asked that they introduce themselves to the rest of the children.

It was plain to see that Mary Lou did not mind being in front of the class. She spoke right up, "I'm Mary Lou Brown. I'm seven years old and in the first grade."

Ben's face was turning red, but he stood tall as he followed Mary Lou's lead. "I'm Ben Brown, and I'm in the sixth grade."

Sister Anne showed them to their seats and proceeded to tell the other pupils what to do. Then she shuffled through papers on her desk, looking for some information about these new students. She was not happy about taking on new students in the middle of the school year.

It would have taken something out of the ordinary to make Sister Anne happy on almost any day. She had looked forward to being a teacher, imagining herself in a bright, sunny room teaching second grade in a large elementary school. Instead, here she was in a one-room school, out in the "country," teaching seven grades all on the same day. How she had longed for the dioceses to close the school, as there were only twelve students in all. But for some reason unknown to her, the school was considered necessary and remained open.

Sister Anne handed Mary Lou a book and told her to learn the names of the continents and the oceans. "I will be around later to hear you recite." She did not suppose the child even knew what a continent was. Therefore, she was somewhat taken aback later in the day, when Mary Lou recited her lesson perfectly and could locate each continent and ocean on the globe.

Meanwhile, she turned to the young boy. "Let's see what you can do, and then I will decide where to place you."

The other children were openly watching Ben as Sister Anne marched to the blackboard and put a long division problem on the board. The older boys looked at one another in amazement as she kept adding figures to the problem. They would have been hard put to even try to work such a long one.

"Let's see you work the problem and then prove your answer."

Ben looked at the board and then he looked at Sister Anne. "I can't," he finally mumbled.

"You can't? Why can't you?" Sister Ann tried to keep a note of aggravation out of her voice, but at the same time, a tiny feeling of satisfaction found its way into her heart. She did not like these new people who were coming into the county. They were all just a bunch of rag-tag hillbillies and probably couldn't even read or write. She did not want to admit that there probably was not one pupil in her school who could have worked the problem she put on the board.

"We had not begun long division in our school," Ben replied.

"Very well, we will try something a little easier. Perhaps a fifth grade problem will be one you can do." She thumbed through the arithmetic book she held in her hand and put up another problem, a written one this time.

The other children snickered as Ben read the problem. He made no move to work it out.

"Do you understand what you have just read, or do I need to read it for you?" Sister Anne also heard the sounds of the other children's laughter, but she made no move to correct them. She looked at Ben and held the piece of chalk out to him, but he just stood there, shifting from one foot to the other. She noticed him double his fists so no one could see his hands trembling.

Sister Anne did not know where to turn. She wondered if this boy really did not know how to do arithmetic problems or if he was just being stubborn. She had no way of knowing he had never seen a nun before and that her habit, with its wide white bonnet, frightened him as much as all the unwanted attention from her and the class.

"Very well, you may be seated. We will have to start you in the third grade. You may listen to the other children as they do their lessons, and I will hear you read this afternoon."

A red-faced Ben sat perfectly still until the bell rang for the students to go home for lunch.

Ben did not wait for Mary Lou, as he knew he was supposed to do. He ran across the meadow and burst into the kitchen door, slamming it with a bang. "I'm not going back there! I'm not!"

"What in the world is the matter?" Mae asked.

Eileen echoed her mother's question, wondering what could be the cause of this outburst.

Ben flopped down at the table, not saying a word.

Mary Lou soon arrived with her hat in her hand and only one glove on. "Mama, I'm in the first grade, but Ben is in the third."

"What do you mean? What happened?"

Ben put his head down on the table and cried so hard he could not talk.

Mary Lou was not a bit shy about telling all that happened and was very dramatic in the telling. "Sister Anne almost made Ben cry. And the other kids laughed at him."

Ben cried even louder.

Mae and Eileen looked at each other. They were at a loss to know what to say. It was a great relief when Avery walked in the door. He was expecting dinner, but instead was greeted with his youngest son sobbing as if he never would stop, while his little sister kept trying to console him.

"Could someone tell me what is the matter? Is Ben sick?"

Eileen and Mary Lou began talking at the same time.

Avery held up his hand. "Just a minute. Ben, since this seems to be about you, why don't you tell me what it's all about?"

Ben lifted a tear-streaked face and managed to tell how Sister Anne had made him look stupid in front of the whole school. *And*, how she had demoted him to the third grade.

Avery sat down on the bench by his son and drew his head over onto his shoulder.

"Do I have to go back, Daddy?" quavered Ben.

"Well, Son, I'll see what I can do. Now don't think about it anymore. Let's just eat our dinner. I've got a lot of work I have to take care of. You stay home this afternoon and help your mother."

He turned to his daughter, "Eileen, sounds like there has been some misunderstanding. Maybe you had better drop a note to Sister Anne and straighten her out about the Brown family." Eileen grinned and gave Daddy a hug. He knew she could not say all she wanted to in front of the children, but she happily could "straighten out" Sister Anne. Eileen had enjoyed wonderful school days and happy relationships with her teachers. It was obvious from her expression that she could not imagine one of them behaving toward a student as this teacher had done.

By the time Mary Lou was ready to return for the afternoon classes, Eileen's letter was ready.

When Mary Lou arrived at the school, Sister Anne greeted her at the door. It had been an uneasy hour for her. She was not proud of herself for humiliating the young boy. The realization that she had done so deliberately, made her cringe. Surely she would have to go to confession on her way home. Meanwhile, she would try to be kinder to him when the afternoon classes began.

"Where's your brother?" she asked

"He's not coming," Mary Lou answered in a low voice. She held out the letter hesitantly, obviously not quite sure how Sister Anne would respond. Then she quickly went to her seat and whispered quietly, "Please don't be angry with me."

Far from being angry, Sister Anne took the letter with great curiosity. The beautiful handwriting on the envelope sharpened her interest. What could someone who was willing to live in such a rundown house like the one across the meadow have to say to her? She looked at her name again and realized that despite the years she had spent practicing her penmanship at the convent, she never would be able to write as well as whoever wrote the letter.

Sister Anne sat down and opened the letter. Mary Lou watched with great curiosity as the color slowly drained from Sister Anne's face. By the time her teacher reached the end of the letter, her face was as white as the large headdress she wore. Mary Lou wondered if she was crying.

Sister Anne turned as if to lay the letter down on her desk, but instead, she slowly lifted the lid on the little pot-bellied stove that heated the schoolroom. She dropped the letter into the flames and, reaching for the envelope, let it follow the letter.

Straightening her shoulders, Sister Anne rapped on her desk, calling the children to order. Ben's name was never mentioned again.

Mary Lou did not know what her father did, but the next morning, Ben got on the big school bus with Riley and Garvin and continued in the sixth grade for the remainder of the school year.

CHAPTER 5

Letters

*E*ILEEN SAT AT the kitchen table thinking about
her older siblings, who had left home a few years
before. Her eldest brother, Foster, still lived in North
Carolina. He was working in a hardware store and living
with Mae's older brother. From all they had heard, he was
doing quite well. Her older sister, Faye, was attending
nurses training school in Detroit, Michigan, while living
with Avery's brother.

Mae had suggested that Eileen write Faye and Foster
with news of their new home and mailing address. She
was anxious to hear from them and knew Eileen wanted
to hear from her sister.

Eileen quickly dispatched a short letter to her
brother. She instinctively felt that Foster was too
wrapped up in himself to care much about his family.

She wrote about how hard Daddy was working and that everyone was doing their best to adjust to life in their new situation. Having disposed of that duty, she turned with happy anticipation to the letter to Faye. How she missed her! She wrote:

Dear Sister Mine,

How is life in the big city? Are you having as much fun as you thought you would? Have you met any handsome doctors? Tell me all the details. Try not to make me too jealous.

I can't begin to tell you how shocked Mother was when she saw the house we are living in. To describe it best, I would have to say it is an early log cabin propped up by an addition that never has seen a drop of paint. The inside is better than the outside, and if you know Mother, it will end up being a place of peace and rest for all of us. I am trying to help her see the little things that can be done. And that takes some doing, as it really is a dump! Thank heaven for wallpaper and paint.

Christmas is right around the corner, and money is tight. Maybe I should say it is non-existent. The expense of moving took all of Daddy's cash, and he will not have a payday until the first of January. I have to prepare Mary Lou for the fact that she will not be receiving a lot of presents this year. She is a pretty big girl for her age, and I think she will make the best of it. Mother feels bad, but there's nothing to be done; so we will just make do. The day will soon pass.

Eileen continued her letter, retelling the events of the past days, including the story of Ben's ordeal at the school and Granny's dismay at having to climb the stairs to get to her room.

Granny is still the same as far as being set in her ways, but there are some subtle changes. I think the trip up here and all the changes have taken a toll on her health. I miss the sparkle in her eyes sometimes, and I notice that Mother watches her with more concern than usual. It must be hard to get older. You would know more about that than I, seeing as you are older! Hah!

We have had a new addition to the family. Don't panic; it's only a davenport. Dad's cousin, who brought our stuff from Grassy Creek, came by on his way to an auction. Daddy went with him and came home with this big, long, horsehair davenport. It opens up into a double bed. But there's just one hitch. It's so heavy it takes two people, plus a mule, to open it up. Anyway, it's a place for us to sit. He also bought a washtub full of stuff, including two pictures painted on glass. Not bad. I think they will look good, once I get a chance to clean them up.

Faye, you will be shocked to learn that you have a sneak for a sister. Since I am the one who goes across the highway to the mailbox every day, I took a circular that came addressed to "Resident" and hid it. It is an advertisement for a business college in a nearby city. They teach typing, shorthand, book-keeping, and other secretarial skills. The graduates are guaranteed a job.

You are not the only one who wants to have a life of your own. I know Mother needs me right now, and I am willing to help her all I can. But there will be a time when I must go out on my own, and this sounds like a good thing to me. Sooo, I answered the ad and mailed in an application! I know I should have talked it over with Mother and Dad, but you know full well Dad's thoughts on the matter. However, I want a career, too! I want to keep up with my big sister!!

Write to me immediately, but watch your words, and don't spill the beans on me!

Love, your sneaky sister

January 15, 1936
Dear Faye,

I am so mad at your brother that I could spit nails! The other day, Mother and I were in the middle of putting up some curtains when someone drove into the yard and started honking the horn. I went to the door, and there stood Foster and Aunt Lily! Can you believe it?! Without having the courtesy of letting us know they were coming, and without giving Mother time to get the house in order, here they came. I think if Mother could have gone through the floor, she would have. But you know Mother. She pulled herself together and made them welcome. I hurried to the kitchen to start things for dinner.

Foster had come to tell us that he was getting married. He stated that he knew Mother and Daddy could not come to the wedding so he did not want them to feel left out! Can you believe the gall? He did not invite them or give them the opportunity to decline. I could have gladly smacked him! Bless Jo! She started to cry, giving Mother a reason to leave the room and time to change her clothes to be more presentable to Aunt Lily.

Daddy came home at his usual time for dinner and greeted the unexpected guests as warmly as if we had been waiting for them to arrive.

We put dinner together, and regardless of what Aunt Lily thought of our surroundings, she did justice to the meal. Foster, of course, ate heartily and never stopped talking about his new position as manager of the hardware store and his bride-to-be. She is an elementary school teacher. They are purchasing a little brick house to start their married life. You should have seen the way he looked around all the time he was eating, as if comparing his good fortune with that of his poor mother!

Daddy excused himself and returned to his work, saying he would see them at supper. This gave Foster an opening to say they would not be staying, as he was expected back at work as soon as possible. He went outside with Daddy. I would love to know what they said to each other, but when Foster came back inside, his face was pale. It was not long before he suggested they leave.

Aunt Lily cried when she said "good-bye." She remarked about how she could not bear the thought of Mae living in such conditions. The tears angered Mother, but ever being the lady, she reassured Lily that she was perfectly happy and invited her to return at any time.

I think that visit was a turning point for Mother. She looked around and seemed to see the possibilities of even this old house. She told me later that after she got over her anger at Aunt Lily's tears, she determined to make a new life, with no need for pity and no unpleasantness within these walls. She stated that she would welcome every person who came! The love and hospitality she would offer would make up for the looks of the place! She would not be ashamed of our home ever again!

Dear sister, I pray that I will have the grace and fortitude of our mother. By the way, have you said any prayers lately?

Write soon.

Love, Eileen

CHAPTER 6

Neighbors and Friends

*M*AE OPENED THE back door and surveyed the surrounding area. Mr. Wilson's little store was located on the opposite corner of the highway from their house. Avery had set up an account with the storekeeper so that purchases could be paid for at the end of the month. Not that Mae needed much, but there was always a time when one must buy salt, sugar, and other staples.

Spring was arriving. The air still had a slight nip, reminding everyone that winter had not entirely gone away. Off in the meadow, Mae could see a bright yellow dandelion, a sure sign that warmer weather was on the way. Lots of folks disliked dandelions and would dig them up at every chance. But Mae welcomed the sight of the brilliant gold after the dreary gray of winter.

Avery appeared, driving his wagon behind a team of white mules, back and forth across the field on the other side of the highway, spreading manure as he went. He would be bringing his next load from the barn to spread over their garden. The odor would linger in the air for several days.

Mae had to laugh. One could tell the seasons of the year simply by opening the door. Spring in farm country not only had the smell of new growth but also of the fertilizer provided by the animals for distribution on the fields. Summer brought the smell of blossoms and the sound of bees. Burning leaves, over-ripe fruit, and golden rod marked the fall and approaching winter, when the odor of wood burning fires from chimneys across the land would fill the air.

This morning was definitely a spring morning. Mae turned to re-enter the house. Suddenly a movement beside the house caught her eye. She waited, but nothing happened. She had just started to enter the door when a young boy stepped into view, causing her to stumble.

"I'm hongry!"

Mae gazed in astonishment at the creature standing before her. He was skin and bones, dressed in ragged pants at least two sizes too small, even for his thin frame. Mae shivered at the sight of his threadbare shirt. He did not have on a coat or even a sweater, and the temperature warranted at least one or maybe both.

"I'm hongry!" he repeated, twisting his bare arms around his head.

"Who are you?" Mae asked, just as Mary Lou opened the door on her way to school.

"Oh, Mother, that's just Freddie. He probably is hungry. His family hardly feeds him at all." She went on her way as unconcerned as if this young boy was a common sight to her.

Mae quickly filled a plate with leftover biscuits and some sausage and set a large glass of milk on the porch railing. To her surprise, the boy grabbed the food and ran into the nearby woods on the far side of the garden. His shoes, with no laces, flopped up and down on his bare feet.

This all happened so quickly that Mae was not sure it really had taken place. Imagine her surprise later in the day when she found the plate and glass, sparkling clean, sitting on the porch railing. She had a lot of questions for Mary Lou as soon as she came back from school.

Mary Lou was glad to be in the spotlight for a few moments and readily told her mother and Eileen all that she knew about Freddie. It seemed his family lived directly across the road from the school, and one of his sisters came to school; although, she had a difficult time learning. Her name was Mary, also.

"Are there other children?" Mae asked.

"Yes, Mary has a little sister and a baby sister. And then there is Freddie. They don't like Freddie very much.

He wets in his bed, and his mother has to punish him. They don't let him eat at the table with them, and they don't always save any food for him. That's why he is always hungry."

"But why does he run away with his food?

Mary Lou looked at her mother, surprised that she didn't seem to understand. "Because, if he took the food home, they would take it away from him, and then he would still be hungry."

"How is it that you know Freddie?" Eileen inquired.

"I don't," answered Mary Lou, "but I've heard all about him."

"And where did you hear 'all about him'?"

"Mrs. McClosky told me all about the whole family. She knows all about everybody. All you have to do is ask her."

Mother did not think it wise to encourage Mary Lou to repeat gossip when there was no way to verify what she had heard. "Finish your dinner, and hurry back to school. It's time for the bell to ring, and you must not be late."

That night, after the children had gone to bed, Mae related the story to Avery. It seemed that he knew about this family from Mr. Wilson, the storekeeper. The Dorn family was well known to everyone living in the area.

"What about the father and mother?" Mae wanted to know. She never had heard of anybody living like they were.

"Well, Mae," Avery shared what he had learned. "It seems the whole family is mentally handicapped. The father works for WPA, or I don't know how they would survive. He can't read or write, but he is proud of his job. Mr. Wilson says he loves his family and sees nothing wrong with the way they live. People in the neighborhood try to help out, but they won't let anyone help very much."

"How about the one named Freddie?" Mae persisted.

"It seems that he is the eldest and the most severely challenged. They have no idea how to care for him, and I think they are hoping he just will go away somewhere. He mostly hides out in the woods and scrounges for food from anyone who will feed him."

Neither she nor Avery had ever been in contact with anyone who had mental disabilities before and had no one to care for them. Even the poorest of families took care of their own. Neither Avery nor Mae knew what they could do. But Mae felt strongly that someone should do something. She had a long discussion about the matter with her heavenly Father that night, and the discussion continued when she set out a plate for Freddie the next morning.

A few days later, Mr. Wilson told Avery that the social worker from the county had been up to the Dorn household and brought some clothing for the family. She had offered to take Freddie to the county home, but

Mr. Dorn would not hear of it. Without the parents' permission, the county could do nothing.

Perhaps someday things would change and provisions for those kinds of unfortunate people could be made. In the meantime, no one seemed to know what to do or how to improve matters. Therefore, they were simply left alone and tolerated.

Mae was amazed at how many people living in the county came from the south. Each time they went to church, they either met someone whom they had known at one time or someone whose relatives they knew. Hardly a Sunday went past that they were not invited to someone's home for dinner. Mae reciprocated by inviting friends into their home. No one refused, and no one seemed to notice that the house looked like it was ready to fall down, which surprised her.

They became good friends with the Cochran family, who lived within walking distance of their house. Avery and Mr. Cochran had much to talk about, mostly farming. The difference between them was that Mr. Cochran owned his farm, while Avery was merely a renter.

The two families almost had matching children as far as ages went. Permission was granted for one of the girls, who had become good friends with Eileen, to come and spend the night. That evening at supper,

Mae noticed the young girl kept scratching the top of her hand.

"What's wrong with your hand, dear?" she asked.

"Oh, it's nothing. I have eczema. It comes and goes, and I think it is from something that I eat."

Nothing more was said, and the girls went upstairs to talk and giggle before they went to sleep. Eileen had made a pallet on the floor for Mary Lou so that her friend could share the bed in which Eileen and Mary Lou usually slept.

A few days letter, Mae noticed that Eileen was scratching her arms and had a tiny, red rash. It seemed that Mary Lou had the same problem.

Uncle Carl came to visit one afternoon, and Mae showed him the rash. Should she take Eileen to the doctor? None of the home remedies she had on hand seemed to help.

Uncle Carl looked at the rash and burst out laughing. "Mae, you have a first grade class of the seven year itch. You don't need a doctor. You need a few bottles of a sulphur mixture to get rid of these little mites that get under the skin and lay their eggs. Who have you been shaking hands with?" He was having a good time watching the dismay on the faces of Mae and Eileen, and even on Mary Lou. The itch was something that happened only to the dirtiest of people.

"You may think this is funny, but I clearly do not! What am I going to do?"

"I'll go to the drugstore and get something to take care of it," Uncle Carl declared, laughing as he left.

When he returned with two big bottles of a yellow-looking solution, they built up the fire in the kitchen stove and sealed the doors and windows as tightly as they could. Riley brought in the big galvanized wash tub and filled it with hot water from the stove.

Mae shooed everyone out of the room, except Eileen and Mary Lou. When she poured some of the solution into the hot water, a thick cloud of evil-smelling vapor filled the room. The odor, like that of rotten eggs, permeated the house. It was enough to make one gag. After giving orders to Eileen to sit in the hot water until it got cool, Mae made her exit.

When Eileen was finished, the tub was refilled, and Mary Lou took her turn.

As if that were not enough, this scene had to be re-enacted the next day. But the cure worked, and no more cases of "eczema" occurred.

Avery learned that Mr. McCloskey was ill and went to visit to see if he could be of any help. Gus McCloskey had helped him by working on the farm from time to time. Avery liked the fellow, even if he had trouble understanding his thick Irish brogue.

Mary Lou went along, carrying a loaf of home baked bread, fresh from the oven. She and Mrs. McCloskey became friends in no time, and Mary Lou was invited to come any afternoon and have cookies and tea.

The tenant houses of most farms were not usually located close together and since everyone was busy, there was little time for visiting back and forth. Even the children were kept busy with chores and schoolwork. There were no children living near the Brown family except the Dorn family and they were not allowed to have any contact with any of the neighbors. This left Mary Lou without playmates, so she took advantage of this invitation on many afternoons.

Mrs. McCloskey and Mary Lou learned quite a bit from each other. Mrs. McCloskey took it upon herself to educate Mary Lou about all things Catholic. But she was just as quick to inquire about the people called Baptists.

What Mary Lou did not know for sure, she made up, explaining things as she thought they should be. Sometimes she went home and asked her mother or father about the things she did not understand, returning the next day to straighten it out.

Mrs. McCloskey was especially interested in the way the Baptists went down to the creek and what they did there, something called "baptizing." When these occasions occurred, cars stopped to check out what was happening. People got out of their cars and stood on the bridge to watch what they did not understand. Other cars lined the highway or drove over into the meadow. She questioned Mary Lou about it at great length.

"Well," Mary Lou tried to explain, "that's where the preacher baptizes the people who ask Jesus to come into their heart. Mother says the way we baptize is a picture of the death, burial, and resurrection of Jesus. When the preacher puts you under the water, it shows that Jesus was buried. When he lifts you out of the water, that's when Jesus rose again. We don't have a place to bury people under the water, so we gather at the creek to do that." Mary Lou was getting in over her head, and she did not know what to say when Mrs. McCloskey laughed.

"Suppose a turtle gets a hold of your toe?"

"I guess you would holler." Mary Lou laughed along with her friend and was relieved when Mrs. McCloskey suggested some tea and cookies. Mother did not mind her having tea the way Mrs. McCloskey fixed it, with lots of cream and a little tea.

Mr. McCloskey did not get well. Avery learned of his death and went to see if there was anything he could do to help. The funeral was to be held at the McCloskey's home. The casket was placed in the parlor or "front room" until time to proceed to the place of burial. When time for visitors came, he and the boys went to pay their respects. The boys and the friends and neighbors went home, but Avery stayed. About eleven o'clock, Mrs. McCloskey, being an outspoken lady, suggested that he go home so that she could go to bed.

A red-faced Avery explained that where he came from, men would sit up with the body until morning, out of respect for the widow.

To which Mrs. McCloskey replied, "Well, Gus and I were married thirty-seven years, and in all that time, he never hurt me. So I don't think he'll bother me now. I thank you, but I want to go to bed." And so saying, she escorted him to the door.

Eileen was passing through the living room when she heard a brisk rap at the door. Mae was just coming out of the bedroom with Jo in her arms. She was hesitant about opening the door since there was no car in sight.

At the repeated knock at the door, Mae peeped through the curtain and saw a young man dressed in a bowl-shaped hat and a long, black overcoat that reached well below his knees. He seemed pleasant enough, and she did not see any baggage, so he must not be a salesman. He was too well dressed to be a hobo. She nodded to Eileen to open the door.

A pleasant-faced young man removed his hat and introduced himself. "Good morning. I am Father Malone, from the church up on the hill. I just stopped by to welcome you to our community."

"Thank you," Eileen replied. "Won't you please come in? It is really cold this morning."

Father Malone gladly stepped into the warmth of the living room. He explained that he was the priest of the church they could see from their front door and would welcome them to attend services at any time they were able.

"Thank you, but we are Baptist and will be attending the church of our own faith as soon as we get a car. Our neighbors have been very kind to carry us for the present."

"That's fine. Any time you find yourselves without transportation, feel free to visit with us. It's good that we are within walking distance. I think you will find we worship the same God, but perhaps in a little different way. Now I must be going, and I thank you for allowing me in your home. If you ever need me, remember, I am just a few steps away."

Good-byes were exchanged, and Eileen and Mae watched as he strode across the highway and on toward the church.

"What a nice young man," Mae exclaimed. "I bet his church folk really like him. Maybe we will visit his church someday."

That evening as they shared around the supper table about the events of their day, Avery told about meeting the young priest outside the barn that morning. Apparently he had been down the road visiting one of his parishioners. "I liked the young man. He seemed very sincere and was most interesting to talk to. I hope to see him again. Mae, I bet he would enjoy one of your home-cooked meals one evening."

The talk turned to the differences between the Catholic and Baptist religions. Mary Lou, as usual, was full of questions. There were no Catholic churches in Grassy Creek, and this was the first contact the children had ever had with anyone other than Baptists or Methodists.

"Why do they dress so funny? And why do they call him 'Father'?"

"Mary Lou," Daddy tried to explain. They don't dress 'funny.' They dress as they do because it sets them apart and identifies them as special servants of God. It is like a uniform that a nurse or a soldier might wear. People who see them know immediately they are Catholics and are working for the Lord.

"They call their priest 'Father' just like we call our ministers 'Pastor.' He looks after them just like an earthly father looks after his children. We expect our pastor to look after the people of our church like a shepherd looks after his sheep. I think we will find we are more alike than we are different, but sometimes little differences cause big separations. Now I think we had better separate for homework and then bed. Four o'clock comes early!"

In less than a month, Avery came into the house with word that the young priest had died during the night from some unexpected and unexplained cause. Mrs. McCloskey had sent word and announced that they were welcome to go to the funeral services with her, if they so desired.

Eileen stayed home with Jo so that her mother and father could go with their neighbor. The church was packed with both parishioners and clergy from surrounding churches. Many higher church officials came from Baltimore to officiate in the service for one of their own. Avery and Ella Mae did not understand all of the service, most of which was spoken in Latin, but they understood they could pray and thank God for the brief time they had known this young man.

CHAPTER 7

Cars, Chickens, and Peaches

$\mathcal{S}$PRING PASSED SLOWLY, with more adjustments than they had expected. There were a lot of things to get used to in this new phase of life.

The first thing Avery realized was that they could not be without transportation. He needed someone to help him buy a car, make a good selection and see that he was not taken advantage of. He made arrangements for Carl to go with him to town to make this big purchase. Carl would also be the best one to teach him how to drive. Riley and Garvin really wanted to go, but Avery insisted they not miss school.

The day came for Avery and Carl to go to town. That afternoon, Mae stood looking at the clock. It would be time for the school day to end soon and the evening milking to begin. It was not like Avery to be late. Could he have overlooked the time? It was not only growing late, but it looked and felt like snow.

Just as the first soft flakes began to fall, she heard the horn. Avery pulled off the road and came to a stop with a jolt. Uncle Carl got out of the car, grinning and wiping his brow like he was glad to be alive. Mae and Eileen grabbed their coats and went outside to look at the new car, a green 1935 Chevrolet. They looked and then hurried back into the warm house.

Just then, the school bus stopped, and the boys came rushing off, not bothering to come into the house. They wanted to see the car! Mae had to remind them to come in and change their clothes, as it was time to go to the barn. Reluctantly, they left their inspection and got ready for work.

Uncle Carl reminded Avery that he would have to have a license before he could drive on the highway. He agreed to show him all the things he would have to know and promised to go with him for the driving test as soon as he was ready.

The snow was light and did not stick to the ground. Mae was glad. She hoped this would be the last one of the season. As long as it stayed cold, work on the farm was slow.

Avery used the next several days to learn all the ins and outs of driving a car. He opened a gate to the meadow across the road and drove across the highway and onto the grass. He drove up and down several times to get accustomed to the wheel and practiced starting, stopping, backing up, and turning around. By the time they needed to go to town and to church on Sunday, he wanted to have things under control.

The boys went over every detail with their dad. Each one had to sit behind the wheel, even Ben. But Avery was not quite ready to teach them how to drive.

Two weeks later, after he had acquired his first driver's license, Avery parked the car beside the house and went inside to receive congratulations from all the family. He said he felt like a new man.

As soon as the work was done the next Saturday morning, Avery decided the men in the family all needed haircuts, and the boys quickly agreed. They piled into the car, Avery let the clutch out, and with a lurch and a jerk, off they went.

The family arrived home about the middle of the afternoon, with much blowing of the horn and grinning from ear to ear. Behind them came a pick-up truck loaded with strange crates and boxes. Avery opened the front door for the men to roll a large crate into the kitchen, standing proudly to one side while they unpacked an electric washing machine!

Mae could only stare as the men demonstrated how it worked. Avery had explained to Mae that they had to wear white coveralls when they were milking the cows and that this would require a clean pair every day for each of them. She had begun to dread wash day. But now, even though they had to pump the water and heat it on the stove, the burden would be much, much lighter. She watched as the men finished up and then carried in a smaller box and set it on a table. They could open that later.

As soon as the men left, Mae had some questions. "Avery, where did you get the money for all of this? I hope you didn't go into debt. Everything is nice, but it could have waited."

"Well, I have to make monthly payments on the car, but we have to have a way to get around. We can't depend on the neighbors forever. As for the washing machine and the other things, Mr. Jenkins introduced me to a man in town who has a secondhand store. He helps people with what they need until they get on their feet."

"And how much does it cost to get on our feet?" Mae was leery of anything that put them in debt. She did not want Avery's first paychecks to be spent before he got them.

"Now, Mae, you have to let me take care of things like that. I promise not to buy anything we can't pay for after we get settled. I have arranged with Mr. Wilson that we can charge any groceries we need until the first of each month, and then I will settle with him."

Mae knew from the tone of his voice that no more was to be said about the matter.

Avery picked up the little box that had been placed on the table and, like a child with a new toy, carefully opened it. He was very deliberate in his movements, so much so that Mae wanted to grab it and rip it open herself. What had he bought this time? She was not used to surprises and found it hard to wait for him to lift a little, brown box out of all the packing material. He placed the box on the table, unwound a long cord, and plugged it into an electrical socket in the wall. Static and weird noises issued forth, and as Avery turned some knobs on the front of the box, a man began speaking. Avery had bought a radio! He sat back as pleased as if he had just purchased the end of all their dreams.

After supper was over, they all gathered around while he played with the knobs until strains of music reached their ears. They listened to The Grand Ole Opry from Nashville, Tennessee, with great enjoyment. Mae especially like the song one of the men, Roy Acuff, sang. It was called "The Great Speckled Bird." Each time they listened to that program and heard the song, they tried to guess what, or who, the great speckled bird could be. They never did figure it out, but they liked the tune, so they continued to listen.

Avery and the boys liked to listen to the sports programs. They remembered walking to the grocery store in Grassy Creek to listen to the boxing match between Joe Lewis and Max Schmelling and cheering when Lewis won. Joe Lewis was black, but he was an American, and they were happy that he was the winner. Now they could not only hear the boxing matches but also baseball and other games, right from their own living room.

In the evenings, they could hear the mellow voice of a newscaster, Lowell Thomas, as he brought reports of what was happening around the world. It became a nightly ritual that as soon as the dishes were done and homework was completed, everyone listened to the news and then went to bed.

Mae missed her chickens. When Avery brought her the first sprig of pussy willow blossoms, signifying spring had arrived, she urged the boys to clean out the chicken house. Avery ordered fifty baby chickens through the mail, and the day the postman left a card in the mailbox saying they had arrived, Avery went to the post office and picked them up.

It seemed odd to hear peeping sounds coming from the big cardboard box Avery carried into the house. He gently set the box down close to the stove. Mae and Eileen gathered around while he cut the tape off the box and lifted the lid. Little, fuzzy, yellow balls lifted their heads, and all of them seemed to peep at one time. Mae held Jo in her lap as she lifted one of the little chicks close enough for Jo to touch it. Jo gave a delighted laugh and grabbed the yellow fluff before Mae could stop her.

Only quick action on her mother's part saved the little chick from being squeezed to death.

Half of the little chickens were moved into the lid, and arrangements were made for food and water to be placed in the bottom of each box. Now the little ones could move around. Mae and Eileen picked them up, one by one, and snapped off a little piece of hard shell attached to the end of each beak. That hard crust had been necessary for them to peck their way out of the shell when they were hatched, but now it was no longer needed. It always amazed Mae that the chicks did not need to be taught how to eat or drink, and she marveled again at the wonder of a Creator God who left nothing to chance but caused all things to work in perfect order. How could anyone not believe in God when they watched the miracles of creation?

The children were as excited as their mother when they came in from school and saw the boxes of baby chickens. Each one had to hold a little chick and invariably rubbed the soft, yellow fuzz against his or her cheek. Mae put a little of the shredded packing material in the bottom of each box. They laughed as the little ones began to scratch around as if looking for something to eat. Mae did not miss this opportunity to speak about the marvel of God's creation and the wonder of His love and provision for even these little ones.

Avery built a little coop and fenced in a small pen so that the young chicks could be moved out of the house to their own surroundings. At first they huddled together for warmth, but soon a few adventurous ones ventured out of the coop onto the grass. It did not take long for the others to follow. As they grew, they would be moved into the chicken house and larger chicken yard. Mae hoped they would lay some small eggs by the end of summer.

Avery was proud of the apple trees he had planted in Grassy Creek, and they had enjoyed the fruit from them. There were a few apple trees in the meadow, but apple orchards were closer to the mountains in the western part of the state. So it was a real pleasure to find peach orchards within a few miles of the farm. Although peach trees thrived in this moderate climate, they would not grow in the colder air of the mountains, so their family had never had peaches before.

Avery drove the boys to one of the orchards, where the owner had placed baskets of peaches on a roadside stand for sale. When Avery inquired about the price, he found that cheaper baskets could be had if one wanted to pick up the peaches that had fallen to the ground. He quickly set the boys to work picking up the slightly bruised peaches. He took home several baskets, with the promise to return later for some more.

That evening, the entire family gathered around for a "peach peeling." Mae had a pan of boiling water on the stove. She washed the peaches and dropped a few at a time into the boiling water. After only a minute or so, the peaches were dipped out of the hot water and placed into a pan that was placed on the table. Each family member took a peach and pierced the skin with a small paring knife. The skin easily slipped off the peach. Any bad spots were cut out of the fruit, the peach split in half, and the seed removed. Then the fruit was packed into glass jars that had been washed and scalded and were waiting on the table.

The work moved swiftly, as the peaches were so hot they had to be handled quickly. Of course, each one had to taste a slice or two to make sure the fruit was of good quality. It was no wonder Avery had to make a return trip to the orchard before the season was over. They all knew how good those same peaches would taste for breakfast some winter morning and that they'd be lip-smacking good when served with a slice of Mae's pound cake after dinner on some future Sunday.

Mae canned peaches. She made peach cobbler. She made peach butter. They ate peaches on cereal, on pancakes, with sugar and cream, on ice cream, and any way that peaches could be consumed. It was almost worth the move to Maryland to discover peaches!

CHAPTER 8

Visitors

AS THE WEATHER grew warmer, they became used to seeing men walk up and down the road in front of the house. Many people were out of work, and "hobos" walked from town to town looking for a job or, more often, for food.

If Mae heard a knock on the door, she peeked out the window. When it seemed like someone in need, she handed out a plate of leftover meat and biscuits, accompanied by a large glass of milk or cup of hot coffee. She never opened the door for any of them to enter the house.

Sometimes one would come to the kitchen door and offer to chop wood or do some other menial task in exchange for food. Mae never turned one away without the offer of something. "You never know when you might be entertaining an angel unawares," she would say to whoever was near. She usually quoted the passage from the writer of Hebrews that says, "Do not forget to entertain strangers, for by so doing some people have entertained angels unawares." This verse was a reminder of the stories in the Bible about the times angels visited Abraham and Lot. Neither of the men knew their visitors were angels, but they granted them hospitality just the same.

These unemployed men were not the only ones who went up and down the highway. Men driving dilapidated pick-up trucks often stopped to try to sell leftover scraps of lumber or paint or pipe from building jobs where they had worked that day. Sometimes the builder would let them have remnants of whatever work was being done to help them earn a few extra dollars.

So it was that a truck stopped one evening with the remnants from several rolls of linoleum. After talking with Avery and unrolling some pieces of linoleum to show the pretty patterns, they went into the kitchen to measure the floor space. One piece seemed to fit from wall to wall, except for about fourteen inches along one side. There was no way to make it fit right. Regardless, Avery agreed to give the man ten dollars, provided that he helped put the piece in place.

Since the linoleum piece had to be slipped under the heavy cast iron cook stove, the man hesitated. But he eventually agreed to assist, and the sale was made. They moved the tables and chairs out of the room. Then, using two pieces of 2x4 lumber, they lifted the stove enough to guide the linoleum under the legs. Even with some of the old boards showing on one side, the shiny surface was an improvement in the room. Ella Mae agreed it would be much easier to clean than the wooden floor beneath it.

Mae never told Avery that she had seen a piece of linoleum in the Montgomery Ward catalogue that could be cut to the proper size for just a few dollars more than he'd paid for the partial piece. Avery had his pride, and she would not be the one to make him feel cheated.

Later in the morning, another knock sounded at the door. "My goodness, this is getting to be like Grand Central Station," Mae said as she went to answer it.

A well-dressed, middle-aged man stood at the door. He was carrying an official-looking briefcase. "Good morning. Is this the home of Miss Eileen Brown?"

Mae was obviously surprised to find a stranger asking for their daughter. She nodded her head but did not invite the gentleman in.

"Allow me to introduce myself." The man politely took off his hat and handed Mae a card with his identification on it. "My name is Samuel Taylor, and I am a representative of Thornton's Business College. I received an application from a Miss Eileen Brown to our school, and I wondered if I might speak with her?"

Eileen was listening to this conversation, and suddenly her knees began to tremble. For a moment, she thought she was going to faint. Oh, why hadn't she told Mother about sending in that application? "Yes, Mother," she finally managed to say, "I did send an application, and I meant to tell you about it, but it slipped my mind. I did not know they would be sending someone in person. Please allow Mr. Taylor to come in."

Eileen could see that although Mother was not sure what exactly was going on, she was determined to find out. Her mother invited the gentleman in. Eileen took his coat and showed him to a chair.

Mr. Taylor appeared to be uncomfortable, like he realized that his visit was a complete surprise to the ladies. He seemed somewhat at a loss about how to proceed. He and Mae both looked relieved when Avery opened the kitchen door and entered the room.

Eileen quickly made introductions. Then Mr. Taylor explained that he was recruiting students for the business school that employed him. He continued, "This is a highly-qualified school for young people seeking employment in the secretarial field. We train our students in typing, shorthand, bookkeeping, and all the skills they would need to earn a living."

Avery held up his hand, interrupting the man. "I don't believe we have anyone here who would be interested in what you are selling."

Eileen's heart turned over. "Please, Daddy. Information about the school came in the mail, and it sounded like something that I could do. So I sent in an application. I meant to talk to you and Mother about it, but I really didn't know anyone would come. Please let Mr. Taylor tell you about it."

Avery looked at Eileen with astonishment and then at Mae. "Did you know about this, Mae?"

"No, I am just now hearing about it."

Eileen wanted to cry. She just knew her chances were over and it was all her fault. Why hadn't she said something about wanting to go to school? Why didn't she show the application to one of them?

"Well, Mr. Taylor," Avery looked the man over, "I'm sure your school is fine for those who can afford it, but as you can see, we do not have money right now for such things, even if Eileen wanted to go."

Mr. Taylor stood to his feet and reached for his coat. "Mr. Brown, I realize I have come at a bad time, and I apologize. I would like to tell you that our school is one where you can work while you are learning. I have two other young ladies to interview, so I will be on my way. You folks talk things over, and I will stop by tomorrow on my way out of town. If you want to hear details about the school, I will be glad to talk with you. If not, thank you for your time today. I will leave this catalog with all the information you might need to know, and I'll pick it up tomorrow."

Avery shook hands with Mr. Taylor and walked with him to the door. The door closed, and dead silence followed.

Eileen was almost afraid to look at her father. "I'm sorry, Daddy," she managed to say. She knew that tears would flow if she said another word. She wished her mother would say something. Anything would be better than this silence. But not a word was said, even during their dinner.

Avery sat down to rest a few minutes after they finished eating. He idly thumbed through the catalog Mr. Taylor had left on the table. Finally he said, "I can't sit around here all day. I have work to do, but we *will* talk more about this tonight."

Eileen cleared the remains of dinner from the table while Mae poured herself a cup of coffee and sat down. She had known this time would come, but she was not quite ready to face it. What would she do without Eileen around to talk with? She could do the work. That was not the problem. The problem would be loneliness.

"Eileen, I did not know you wanted to leave so badly. I wish you had talked this over with us. At least we would have had a little warning."

"I know I should have, and I'm sorry. Mother, I miss Faye more than I ever thought I would. Maybe I envy her a little. I just want to do something with my life too, and when I saw that circular, it seemed like an answer to my prayers."

"I understand if you want to go to work and do something for yourself, but I had hoped that you might be satisfied to work at one of the stores in town. I'm sure Mr. Jenkins would be glad to introduce you to some of the shop owners."

"But, Mother, I don't want to work in a store. Not that there's anything wrong with that, but I want to be more than a salesgirl. I want to *do* something."

"I hope you don't become so involved with *doing* something that you don't forget to *be* something!"

"Oh, Mother, please understand. You agreed when Faye wanted to go to nursing school. Won't you help me with Daddy—the way you helped her?"

"Eileen, I don't think you realize how much your father has on his mind right now, and I, for one, will not add to his burdens. Whatever he decides, you must understand he is looking out for what he sees as your best interests."

Jo chose this moment to fret. She was wet and hungry. Mae was relieved to have an excuse to end this conversation. She left to take care of the baby.

Eileen went upstairs with the thought of having a good cry. Instead, she decided to tell her troubles to Granny. Maybe she would have an idea of how to persuade Daddy to let her go to college. Eileen was so caught up in her own trouble that she failed to notice that Granny was not her usual perky self. Without thinking of anything but what she wanted, she launched right into her story.

"Granny, I don't want to work in a store. I want to amount to something! I mean, there's nothing wrong with working in a store, but anybody can do that. I want to do better than that! I want something more than this," Eileen gestured at her surroundings.

Granny gave her an understanding look but took her time before speaking. She worded her reply very carefully, obviously trying not to discourage Eileen or put Avery in a bad light. Eileen knew that Granny had her own disagreements with Avery, but she never would say anything against her son-in-law to one of his children.

"Eileen, nothing will kill your chances quicker than giving your father the impression that you are ashamed of what he has provided for you." She paused again before she spoke. "Why do you want to go to this particular school?"

"It's not just this school, but I know Daddy does not have money to send me to college, and this seemed like a way to get around that problem."

"Do you really want to be a secretary?"

"I don't know if that is what I want to do forever, but it's a start. It's a place to begin so that I can get a good-paying job. Maybe something better will open up after that."

"Then, that's what you should tell your father. He will listen to that kind of talk. He'll be pleased that you want to better yourself, not just get away from home. And for goodness sake, don't say, 'Granny said...'"

Avery said nothing more about the matter until supper was over and he and Mae had spent a few minutes in the bedroom talking.

Eileen was in the kitchen, anxiously waiting for him to open the subject. He looked like he might have enjoyed making her squirm. She busied herself clearing the table of the dirty dishes and putting the leftover food away.

"Eileen, your mother and I have decided to let Mr. Taylor tell us more about the school and answer some of our questions."

Eileen was so surprised at this statement that she could not think of what to say. "Oh, thank you, Daddy. What did Mother say?"

"Just the usual, 'Have you prayed about this?'"

Eileen laughed. "And what did you say, Daddy?"

Avery quoted his favorite verse from Psalm 37:25: "Once I was young and now I am old; yet I have not seen the righteous forsaken, nor his seed begging bread."

Laughter broke the tension of the afternoon, and Eileen went to bed thinking that maybe she would realize her dream of going to college after all.

The next day, true to his word, Mr. Taylor stopped by the house around dinnertime. Avery had been watching for his car and came to the house to greet him. Together the adults gathered around the table, and the discussion began. With cups of hot coffee and the catalogue open before them, Mr. Taylor answered their questions. One of the most important ones was where Eileen would live.

"Our staff has a list of respectable people who will provide room and board to any student willing to do a few chores. This might include helping prepare meals or light housekeeping chores. All of these homes have been thoroughly investigated and approved by our director.

"One other point is that students who graduate with satisfactory grades are guaranteed a job when they finish their course of study. Each course usually takes an equivalent of two years, but a good student who really tries can finish in a much shorter time.

"I am taking the other two girls I mentioned yesterday up to visit the school, and I would be happy to take Eileen and let her examine the situation for herself—if that would be agreeable with you. Of course, I would bring all of them home the same day."

Avery looked at Ella Mae, and they both looked at Eileen.

"Well, since other girls are going along, I guess you might go," said Avery. "If you can convince me it is as good as this man is saying, we might let you enroll. I'm afraid you are getting your hopes up for nothing."

With these words, the tears did flow. Eileen threw her arms around her father's neck and was surprised to find tears on her mother's face as she turned to her. Was it a case of dreams coming true, or of prayers being answered? Eileen realized it was probably a little of both.

CHAPTER 9

Progress and Promises

*A*VERY HAD BEEN elected to be a deacon in the Grassy Creek Baptist Church. He considered the office of deacon one of highest honor, and he always participated in anything that would build up the church. It was only natural that one of the very first things he and Ella Mae did after moving to Maryland was move their church membership. The other men began to observe how he lived, and after a time, this church elected him as one of their deacons. It was an honor he took very seriously.

Mae appreciated the friendship offered to her by the ladies of the church. Most of them came from backgrounds very similar to hers and knew the people and places surrounding Grassy Creek. When they visited back and forth in each other's homes, the time together usually followed a familiar pattern. After a bountiful meal, the men would retire to the living room or a shady porch, where they were soon engrossed in talk about crops, politics, or religion. The women cleaned up the table and kitchen and retired to exchange plant cuttings, quilt patterns, or crochet instructions. Talk usually centered on their children, housekeeping, or gardens.

Mae felt at ease with most of the women she met. She liked the fact that they looked straight at her as she talked. She believed the eyes tell about the people who inhabit the body, and it is in the eyes that people really live and show their feelings. She was not used to speaking of religious things in ordinary conversation. At first when she met Mrs. Wells, who spoke of the Lord as if they were on a first name basis, she was a little uncomfortable. But she soon realized she had met someone fine and unusual. This was someone who would be her friend no matter what.

Eileen finished her studies at Thornton's Business School and found a job immediately. In fact, she simply continued working at the place where she had been employed as a student. She still lived with Mrs. Ebby, the kind widow lady who gave her a room in exchange for a little housework. She hoped to have her own place when she had saved up enough money.

Avery finished the first year of his contract. After a few tense moments, he was able to come to an agreeable settlement with Mr. Jenkins for the next year. The terms of the contract read that Avery was to receive thirty dollars a month and one-third of any profits at the end of the year.

Mr. Jenkins seemed quite surprised that, far from being an ignorant man from the hills of North Carolina, Avery proved to be an astute business man who kept careful records. Avery carried a little notebook from the local feed store in which he recorded every transaction that had bearing on the work of the farm. Every head of livestock bought or sold, all money received from the sale of crops, the cost of any repairs or purchases made on behalf of the farm, and wages that were paid to extra help he hired were carefully noted. In fact, his little account book read like a journal of the past year's work, with the dates and amounts of money involved in each transaction that took place. Mr. Jenkins had to adjust his figures in a few instances, but he could not dispute Avery's records and receipts.

Mr. Jenkins sometimes hinted at the fact that he was getting old and wanted to retire. There was a promise that they would discuss the matter again at the end of Avery's contract next year. Although Avery never had told Mae, he had hopes of one day buying the farm from Mr. Jenkins. Then she could move into the big, white house on the hill. Meanwhile, he would keep his hopes to himself, just in case it didn't work out.

Christmas at the end of 1936 was very different from the year before. There was a pretty card from Foster and his new bride with details of their wedding and descriptions of their house that was "small but adequate." There was a promise of a visit as soon they could arrange time off from work. Mae wondered what Foster had told his bride about the house his parents lived in. Would she be offended, as Aunt Lily had been? Mae determined to welcome and love her as one of the family. The response was up to her.

A beautiful card from Aunt Hazel and Uncle Bill and the children included a hastily written note from Faye, saying she was very busy at the hospital because many people were sick. She said that as many nurses as could be spared wanted to spend Christmas with their families and the student nurses had to fill their shoes. In spite of the extra work, there were many parties to be attended. She would try her best to attend several.

Eileen arrived home for Christmas week loaded down with packages. She brought every kind of decoration that could be found for their tree. Daddy had brought a tall cedar in from the woods beyond the garden. When they had hung all the pretty balls and placed tinsel icicles from the top to the bottom of the tree, there were still a lot of decorations left over.

Mary Lou gazed at the tree and said that she was sure it was the most beautiful tree she had ever seen. Even if there were no presents, it promised to be the best Christmas ever.

Eileen thought it would be nice to decorate a tree for the Dorn family. There was too much good feeling in their home to keep just for themselves. So Mother fixed a nice box of food. Mary Lou helped carry the extra trimmings, and Eileen and she set out on their trek across the meadow.

Eileen was not sure how they would be received, but Mrs. Dorn was happy to welcome them into her home. The furnishings were a mixture of this and that, obviously donated from various sources. However, the house was somewhat clean.

There was a tree standing in the corner but no decorations at all. The two girls set to work, aware that the Dorn children were watching them from behind a flimsy curtain that divided the small room from what Eileen surmised was their bedroom. Soon they were edging out to stare in awe at the way their little tree had been transformed into a thing of beauty. There was no sign of Freddie.

When the tree was finished, Eileen sat on the floor and gathered the children around. She told them the story of the first Christmas, when Baby Jesus was born. She could not tell from their reaction if they ever had heard the story before. They seemed to enjoy the attention, even if they did not grasp the truth of the story.

Mrs. Dorn went into the bedroom and brought out her own new baby and proudly offered to let Eileen hold him. He was wrapped in a very thin blanket and needed his diaper changed. Eileen held him a minute, and then she and Mary Lou said "good-bye." Everyone came to the door as the two girls waved and went thoughtfully back to their warm home.

Later that afternoon, Eileen and Mary Lou took a box of cookies and a pretty shawl to Mrs. McCloskey. It would be her first Christmas alone, and Mary Lou did not want her to feel sad. Mrs. McCloskey served tea and stolen made from a recipe of her mother's. She said that of all the gifts she received, none was more welcome than the big hug from Mary Lou as they left her door.

Christmas morning was a day of gifts of every kind. There were books and a doll and toys for playing house for Mary Lou, a game for Ben, and new clothes for all the family. There also was an electric iron and a glass churn for Mae and a new hat for Avery.

The family crunched into the "Green Hornet," as Avery had dubbed the car after hearing a favorite mystery story on the radio. Then they joined their friends for a worship service that brought their minds away from presents to the reason for Christmas. The reading of the scriptures from Luke's gospel, the prayers of praise and thanksgiving, and the singing of songs that told the story of that first Christmas, set the stage for a joyful day. Every person in church that morning burst into "Joy to the World" at the close of the service.

Before everyone went home, greetings of neighbor to neighbor and friend to friend extended the feeling of good will that heralded great things for the coming year. The Brown family finally began to feel "at home."

CHAPTER 10

Another Summer

SPRING FINALLY RETURNED, and Ella Mae looked forward to the changes she knew were coming. The busy time of spring planting was almost over, and they soon would be waiting and watching as the garden and crops came to life and began to bear fruit. Wild flowers and grasses already had spread across the little orchard between the house and the schoolyard, bringing God's call to her heart and the knowledge that there would be strength for her needs, whatever the needs may be.

Riley and Garvin were going to graduate in May. Riley was making plans to go to college in preparation for the ministry. He no longer preached to the chickens, as he had done in Grassy Creek. He now believed that

God wanted him to preach to people. He needed to prepare himself to do just that.

Garvin, on the other hand, was going into business. Mae sometimes worried about his determination to make money. Her prayer was that he would not allow that to become the sole aim of his life. He and Eileen seemed to be geared alike in their ambitions of wanting to make a success of their lives and all that entailed. There seemed to be little evidence that they were considering God in their plans. That concerned Ella Mae, and she wondered if Avery had noticed their children's attitudes, too.

Eileen now had her own apartment, and Garvin was planning to live with her until he finished school. He already had put in his application at the same school Eileen had attended, Thornton's Business College. He had been accepted and could begin as soon as he was out of high school. He also had lined up a part-time job at a sporting goods store and was counting the days until he could pack his bags and be on his way.

Mae dreaded seeing her family slipping away and yet acknowledged that this was the way life was supposed to be. One generation had to give way to the next.

She thought about her younger children, who were growing quickly, too. Ben would finish elementary school and be ready for high school in the fall. Mary Lou would be in fourth grade, and Jo could not be called "Baby Jo" any longer. She would be two years old in June.

The most noticeable change in the family was with Granny. She seemed to have lost her perky attitude. Many days she preferred staying in her room to spending time with the family. Whenever Ella Mae was in the kitchen, she found herself listening more and more often for a step in the room overhead. Lately she had begun carrying Granny's meals up the stairs.

As time went by, the children noticed that Granny told them the same things over and over again, sometimes within a matter of minutes. She talked about her earlier days as if they were very recent, but she could not remember where she had laid her apron.

Even Avery noticed a change in Granny's thinking. They no longer sparred with their words. Mae noticed that he was being more soft-spoken as he helped Granny in little ways he had ignored before. The whole family became more watchful.

During the hottest days of summer, late July and August, the farmers' work slowed down while they were waiting for harvest time. This was the time for revivals in many churches. Every night for two weeks, an evangelist, or sometimes a pastor from a nearby church, would hold preaching services. Neighbors invited their friends, and everyone hurried to finish their milking and other chores so they could attend these meetings. If the preacher was especially convincing and people were responding to the messages, the revival might be extended an extra week.

It was expected that the deacons and other church members would take turns having the preacher for supper each night. While the wife prepared the meal, the husband would go with the preacher to visit those in the neighborhood who might be candidates for church membership or might not be Christians at all and invite them to the services.

There were two traditions Ella Mae loved from as far back as she could remember—one was the cottage prayer meetings, and the other was the baptisms at the river. One preceded the summer revival, and the other followed it.

For at least one week and usually two before the revival, deacons were busy lining up hosts for cottage prayer meetings. As the name implied, these prayers services were held in homes at various locations near the church. Mae always told Avery to put their names down to host one of the meetings. The atmosphere of prayer prepared her heart for the time ahead and seemed to bring an awareness of God's presence that sometimes got put aside in the busyness of daily living.

As the prayer meetings began, one or two deacons led in a short discussion of a Scripture passage, and then prayer requests were made. These included personal requests for family members, requests for those whom people felt needed to be converted or turned from the way they lived to a belief in Jesus Christ as the one who loved them and had given His life to save them, and requests for those who were ill or in troubled circumstances. When everyone had shared their requests, participants knelt by their chairs or simply bowed their heads, and as many as felt led to pray aloud did so. Others prayed silently. When the leader had given ample time for all the prayers to be said, a final "amen" resounded from the group.

Although it was always stressed that they were meeting to pray and not to eat, the hostess followed the last "amen" with coffee and some kind of refreshment. Mae became known for her apple cake and strong coffee, liberally laced with thick cream.

Following the revival, there was a Sunday afternoon baptismal service in someone's meadow where there was a creek deep enough to plunge the baptismal candidate all the way under the water. None of the church members wanted to miss this meaningful service. The men of the church would set up two "changing" tents at one side of the meadow. The ladies of the church had made special white robes to be put around the women candidates. The men being baptized wore white shirts and washable pants.

When all was ready, the congregation passionately sang "Shall We Gather at the River." Then pastor read a passage of Scripture, usually Matthew 3:13–17, which speaks of Jesus' baptism. The pastor, assisted by a deacon, then walked out into the water and waited as another deacon helped the candidates enter the stream. They were led out into the water until they were about waist deep. One by one, the candidates were asked to give their personal testimonies, telling how they came to know that Jesus had forgiven their sins. Then they were asked if they would promise to live as Christ directed for the rest of their lives.

Mae loved the next part, where the pastor intoned the age-old formula, "Then, led by the power invested in me, my brother (or sister), as Christ was buried to sin (candidate was lowered into the water) and raised to walk in the newness of life (candidate was raised up out of the water), I baptize you in the name of the Father, the Son, and Holy Spirit."

Some came out of the water shouting "Amen!" or "Hallelujah!" Some clapped their hands, some were silent; but all were smiling! Ladies of the church were waiting at the edge of the stream to receive the newly baptized ones; wrap them in big, white towels; and then lead them away to change into dry clothes. When the last person had been cared for, the remaining folks sang "O Happy Day, That Fixed My Choice" to end the ceremony.

All of the baptismal services drew crowds of onlookers. Most came out of curiosity and some out of interest. Larger churches in the city had baptismal pools within their buildings, but Mae always felt they were missing some of the closeness with each other and with God by not being baptized in the open, in the midst of God's creation.

This was also the season for the yearly "tent meetings." Usually a preacher who did not have a church of his own would buy or rent a large tent that would hold a hundred or more people and set it up in someone's meadow. The meadow had to be large enough for the tent and for parking. A piano, pulpit, and folding chairs were made ready for the service.

These meetings usually lasted at least two weeks. If attendance was good (and the offerings were good), they might be extended longer. Here again, the preacher, piano player, and song leader were invited into homes for supper each night. The heat of the "dog days" did not seem to deter those who attended these meetings. A generous supply of fans, usually from the nearby funeral home, was always on hand.

These tent meetings usually were well attended, at least in the first few nights. Some came out of curiosity, and some came who did not usually attend church anywhere. Many came because they loved the Lord and liked the lusty singing of the hymns they had known since childhood. If the preacher was eloquent and touched the hearts of the congregation, some shouted to the Lord and clapped their hands out of joy. Many would go down to the foot of the altar and kneel in prayer for themselves or for someone they felt needed the touch of the Master.

It was here that the term "holy rollers" came into use. The reaction of those who openly expressed their happiness about having their sins forgiven was not understood by those who felt that one's religion should be more restrained and dignified. Like many things that were not understood, exaggerated stories often were repeated and believed.

Ella Mae enjoyed going to these services. It was a chance to meet with other women in the area. They took time away from their busy work of gardening and canning and housework to catch up on news from "back home" or the welfare of folks they did not get to see very often. People from many different churches took this opportunity to get together and hear a preacher different from their own. These meetings furnished events that could be talked over again and again during the coming days and months. The previous nights' services and the singing of other nights were evaluated and commented upon. The success or failure of a meeting often was dependent on whether or not the piano player was good or whether or not the emotions of those attending were stirred. The women remarked that people didn't seem to shout like they used to or that the men were more reluctant to let their amens be heard. The joy of the Lord was something these folks needed to keep them going during the hard times.

Ella Mae's reputation as a good cook did not escape the notice of these visiting preachers. Whether it was during revival time at the church or tent meeting time in the meadow, her table was sure to groan with the produce from her garden, platters of fried chicken, and mounds of fresh butter on hot biscuits or mashed potatoes.

Although many people thought of these revivals as times when un-churched people came into a new relationship with the Lord, most realized that no matter how long one had been a Christian, old fires needed stirring. They all needed to hear the old, old story over again. Somehow it still seemed as thrilling as the first time it ever was heard.

Sometimes those who had been Christians for a long time fell into sin. There was always a call for those who felt a need for confession or rededication of their lives to the Lord. These were invited to come to the altar to make sure all was well between them and the Lord. One preacher stated, "You know what your sins are. This is between you and God. It's nobody else's business."

Even with the busyness of all the revivals and tent meetings and the many changes in the life of the Brown family, one thing remained the same. Aunt Harriet and her girls always made their annual trip to the country to visit Aunt Ella Mae and Uncle Avery. There was, however, a slight difference this year. Aunt Harriet brought David, a young boy about nine years old, from the inner city of Detroit. David's father was dead, and his mother no longer could care for him. She had placed him in foster care until she could get on her feet. Aunt Harriet and Uncle Bill had agreed to take care of him for the summer.

Everyone in the family made David welcome, and he was delighted to be sharing a bedroom with older boys. Ben especially was glad to have another boy among so many girls. Granny had gone to visit her son in Concord, N.C., freeing up her room for Aunt Harriet and the girls. Jean and Janis thought this trip to the country was a great adventure.

The first morning after their arrival, David listened as Riley and Garvin got dressed to go to the barn. Four o'clock was early for him to be awake, but he had not slept well. The old house creaked, and there was the sound of scurrying feet on the roof, not to mention the sound of an animal panting in the yard. He had no way of knowing it was just a dog passing by. He imagined it might be a wolf or some other wild creature.

As soon as Riley and Garvin left the house, he quietly slipped out of bed and into his clothes. Dawn was just beginning to break enough to distinguish objects. He tiptoed out the door, ran to the barn, and watched as the cows lined up and entered the building. They seemed to know just where to go.

As each cow stepped into a stall, a stanchion was fastened around its neck to hold it in place while it was being milked. A large, cup-shaped fixture was in front of each cow's head, fashioned in such a way that when the cow pushed its nose into the cup, water flowed in, allowing the cow to drink its fill. A feed box in front of each cow's head held fresh hay or grain so that the cows could eat. What David did not know was that now that it was summertime, the cows did not need much food, as they ate their fill of grass from the pasture.

David watched as Riley and Garvin each took a bucket of warm water and some clean towels and washed the cows' udders so that no dirt or foreign object would fall into the buckets of milk. When all was ready, Uncle Avery and the boys, in their clean, white coveralls, sat down on three-legged stools, leaned their heads into the side of a cow, and taking a teat in each hand, squeezed until warm milk flowed. The milk hitting the sides of the aluminum milk buckets seemed to pound out a rhythm.

Uncle Avery eventually called David over and tried to teach him how to milk, but no matter how hard he squeezed, nothing happened. To tell the truth, he was a little afraid of the cows. They were awfully big. He preferred watching Uncle Avery shoot a stream of warm milk into the waiting mouth of a big, black-and-white barn cat.

When all the cows had been milked, Riley and Garvin released the stanchions from around their necks and they returned to the pasture. David was surprised that they walked out in single file, just as his class had to walk down the hall at school. Next, the boys hosed down the barn floor so it would be clean for the next milking, which they said would be that afternoon.

David watched as Uncle Avery carried the milk into the dairy and poured it through a big strainer into tall, metal cans that held ten gallons of milk. When a can was full, it was lifted into an ice-cold vat of water to cool. Later in the morning, a big refrigerated truck would stop and take the cans of milk into the city to a large dairy to be pasteurized and bottled.

The last thing Uncle Avery had to do was scrub and sterilize all the buckets and utensils connected with the milking. Only then could they return to the house for Aunt Mae's good breakfast of hot biscuits, sausage, gravy, and eggs.

Another morning, David went to the garden with Aunt Mae and Aunt Harriet as they picked green beans. They picked a big basket full because Aunt Mae wanted to can the beans while they were still young and tender. He helped dig potatoes out of the loose soil and learned how to pick the most tender lettuce leaves and which tomatoes were the ripest. Aunt Harriet bit into a juicy tomato and encouraged him to try one. He took a tentative bite. It was so sweet and good that the entire tomato vanished in no time. The warm juice dripped from his chin. This was his first experience in learning where his food came from and how it grew. He never told anyone, but he once thought potatoes grew on trees, like oranges.

David helped carry the vegetables to the kitchen and laughed as Aunt Harriet kicked off her shoes before she sat down to start preparing the beans. She showed him how to pull the strings off and break the beans into bite size. It was fun for a little while, but he soon got tired of that part of the job.

Aunt Mae washed the beans and packed them into clean, glass jars that were on the table. She put a teaspoon of salt in the top of each jar and then filled it with boiling water before sealing it tight. Each jar had a rubber ring around the top, and then a zinc lid lined with white porcelain was screwed down as tight as it could be. Next, she placed the jars side by side in a large, metal tub on top of the stove. She filled the tub with hot water until the jars were covered. The beans would have to cook for one hour, and then, after they cooled down, they could be placed on the shelves until winter. David never had seen beans that did not come out of a tin can from the store, and the whole process fascinated him.

Supper that night tasted wonderful to the boy from the city because he ate food he had seen grow and had helped to prepare.

One day, all of the children were given an empty jar and told to go up and down the rows of potato vines and pick off the potato bugs. At first, David and Janis and Jean were reluctant to touch these fat, black-and-white-striped creatures that liked to munch on the green leaves. But then Aunt Harriet explained that if they were allowed to eat the potato leaves, there would not be any potatoes to mash or turn into any of the other dishes they loved. Then it became a contest to see who could catch the most. When they turned the leaves of the plants upside down, they sometimes saw small, yellow things attached to the leaves. Aunt Harriet explained these were little eggs that would hatch into more potato bugs if allowed to stay there. Then it became necessary to mash one leaf against another until all the yellow eggs were destroyed. When all the visible bugs had been caught and all the eggs destroyed, the children hurried to the chicken house and served their catch up to the hungry hens.

The one task David did not like was gathering eggs. He did not mind when the nests were empty and all he had to do was transfer the eggs from the nest to his basket. It was another matter when the hen was still on the nest. Mary Lou showed him how to gently slide his hand under the warm feathers and withdraw the eggs, one at a time. But when David reached a tentative hand toward the watching hen and she fluffed her wings, he quickly jerked his hand out, minus an egg. Mary Lou just laughed and reached under the nervous hen and withdrew two brown eggs for her basket.

Each time they gathered eggs, they put scoops of chicken feed into the feeders and fresh water into the drinking fountains before they left the chicken house. The black and white feathered chickens were busily clucking and scratching as the children closed the door and hurried to the house with the eggs they would have for breakfast the next morning. Any extra eggs would be traded to Mr. Wilson for grocery items or maybe used in cooking or perhaps Aunt Harriet would make a chocolate cake for dessert one night.

Every day, immediately after lunch, Aunt Harriet gathered all the children together. She checked their hands and faces. When she was satisfied that they were clean, she sent them to change their clothes. Each of them proceeded to put on their prettiest clothes. Ben and Mary Lou were included in this ritual. Aunt Harriet had brought clothes especially for these occasions, and there were enough items to go around. Each day she changed something about the children's appearances. It might be bright hair bows for the girls or handkerchiefs for the boys' shirt pockets or a different-colored sash or necktie. When all were ready, she lined them up and gave each one a nickel.

The children dropped their coins into their pockets and proceeded to cross the highway and walk the short distance to Mr. Wilson's store. Either Ben or David was selected to open and hold the screen door for the girls to enter. After greeting Mr. Wilson, they walked straight to the display case of ice cream, and then deliberations began as to their choice of flavor for the day.

The first time this happened, Mr. Wilson was astonished as the party lined up in front of him. Each child politely asked for a cone of his or her choice. Then upon receiving the cone, each child paid a nickel and thanked him politely. Then they lined up and walked back to Aunt Ella Mae's to sit down at the table and relish the remains of their treats.

Each day, Aunt Harriet taught them one thing about correct manners. It might be how to use a napkin, how to ask for food to be passed, or how to excuse oneself from the table. When each child could recite the lesson for the day, they were dismissed to change back into play clothes and entertain themselves.

When this continued to happen day after day, Mr. Wilson began to anticipate their coming. After the third or fourth day, he began to give them a double dip for their nickels.

"You don't see children that polite these days," he said, explaining his generosity to Mrs. Wilson.

By the end of the next week, he was adding a dollop of syrup to the ice cream.

"If they stay all summer, we'll go bankrupt," Mrs. Wilson teased.

Nevertheless, the children enjoyed the break in their day, and so did Mr. Wilson. Afternoons usually passed slowly in this quiet country crossroads, and the children were a welcome interruption.

In the evenings, just as the sun began to fade, they caught fireflies in glass jars with holes in the lids. They released them before going to bed.

One day, Mary Lou thought it would be fun to go for a walk. There was a meadow beyond the woods where a small stream meandered along. They came to a fence that separated the pasture where the cows grazed from the woods. Some of the cows were lying down in the shade provided by a clump of trees, while a few were quietly munching the tender grass. One or two were standing in the stream. David walked close to the fence. He wanted to make sure the cows were not going to chase them. In case they might, he wanted to be able to climb back over the fence in a hurry.

Honeysuckle was in full bloom, and Ben showed them how to bite off the end of the blossom and suck the honey from it.

"We're just like the butterflies and the bees," Janis laughed.

David stumbled over a root. This time they all laughed.

"Pick up your feet, David," Mary Lou said.

"Why is it that you and Ben don't stumble like we do?" he asked.

"You are used to walking on pavement in the city, and since the ground out here in the country is very uneven, it will be awkward for you to keep your balance until you get used to it," Ben explained. "You do have to pick your feet up, but you also need to look where you are going. It's easier if there is a path to follow instead of just walking out in the open like this."

101

The afternoon was getting hot, and they were getting tired. Ben suggested they sit on the edge of the little stream and put their feet in the water to cool off. Everyone was in agreement. David, Janis, and Jean had to pull off their socks and shoes, but all Mary Lou and Ben had to do was dangle their feet over the edge of the bank. They had been going barefoot all summer, and their feet had become almost as tough as leather. Aunt Harriet, however, thought the children in her care should wear shoes, and they were in agreement about that.

They rested and watched the little minnows swimming at the edge of the stream. Dragonflies zipped from one spot to the other, making a swoop at the children's heads as they passed by. Soon everyone was ready to head back to the house. They climbed back over the fence and picked some ferns and flowers that grew in the shade.

David looked up and saw a hornet's nest hanging from a tree branch. "What a large bird's nest," he exclaimed. He started to reach for it, but Ben grabbed his arm.

"Don't! That's a hornet's nest. They don't sing, but they surely can sting."

Mary Lou, who David knew was always ready to show off her knowledge, thought this would be a good time to give her city cousins a lesson about bees. She pointed to some clumps of white clover growing near the fence and some honey bees busily going from flower to flower and said, "Look at their legs. You can see how they are covered with white fuzz. That's pollen from the clover, and they carry that back to their hive and make honey like the kind Daddy likes on his biscuits in the morning. That's why they are called 'honeybees.'"

"Do they sting?" Jean wanted to know.

"Yes they do, but it doesn't hurt as much as the hornet's sting."

"Just mind your own business and stay away from the bees and they won't hurt you," Ben advised. He gave Mary Lou a look, like he thought she sounded a little too uppity. "Let's see who can reach the back porch first."

With that, Ben took off running. The others followed suit. They all arrived breathless and tired, ready for supper.

Summer was over all too soon, and Uncle Bill came to take his family and David back to Detroit. David declared that it was the best summer of his entire life.

CHAPTER 11

A Ruined Dream

*A*VERY GATHERED HIS records together and went to meet with Mr. Jenkins to settle their accounts for the year. It also was the end of their contract together, and Avery was confident that he at least would be able to make a bid for the purchase of the farm from Mr. Jenkins. If all went as he hoped, he would be coming home with a big surprise for Ella Mae. He had not mentioned the possibility of buying the farm for fear that Mr. Jenkins would change his mind about selling. But Avery had been observing his boss for the past few months and could not help but see how tired he seemed much of the time.

Full of confidence and anticipation, Avery approached the big, white house. He pressed his hand against his shirt pocket, making sure his checkbook was there. He had saved money toward a down payment and knew he would have no problem selling his little farm in Grassy Creek to get enough to make a deal he could live with.

Mr. Jenkins invited Avery into the house, and they proceeded to the table, where Mr. Jenkins had his records ready. He gave Avery a long look, as if trying to decide what he was thinking. He then shuffled through his papers and seemed to be looking for something, even though he usually had things in perfect order.

"Well, Avery," he began, "let's get the past year's accounts settled first."

Avery was ready, and the two put their figures together. Once again, Mr. Jenkins tried to get the better of Avery on a few items but found he could not argue with the carefully kept records Avery produced. When the final figures were agreed upon, Mr. Jenkins wrote a check and handed it across the table to Avery.

Mr. Jenkins fidgeted with his papers a few minutes and then cleared his throat. "Well, Avery, I guess this is the end of the road for us. You have been a good worker and have been more honest with me than some have been in the past. I wish you good fortune in the year ahead."

Avery was puzzled. "What do you mean? Aren't you going to sell the farm? I'd like to make you an offer, if you are."

"No, Avery, I'm not going to sell the farm. I have given the farm to my grandson, lock, stock, and barrel. He will be taking over the first of the month."

For a moment, Avery did not know what to say. He was stunned! In a moment, all his hopes and dreams simply fled away!

"You won't have to be in a hurry about moving. He will take over the work, but since he lives nearby, he won't be using the house anyway. Probably will just tear it down. So you can take your time about finding another place. I'll give you a good recommendation, of course."

Avery stood, trying to take in all that Mr. Jenkins had just said. There would be no dream to share with Ella Mae. There would not even be a paycheck to share with her. He was out of a job! They were out of a home!

For a moment, white, hot anger flooded his face. If Mr. Jenkins had been a younger man, he would have hit him. Why had he not listened when Claude tried to tell him to watch the man? Why had he not realized that a man who would cheat over the sale of a calf or a bushel of wheat could not be trusted?

From somewhere, a calming spirit suddenly entered his head. "That's OK, Mr. Jenkins. We'll be out by the end of the month, and your grandson can do as he pleases with the house."

As Avery slowly left the room, he turned to quote his favorite Bible verse, "Once I was young, but now I am old and I have never seen the righteous forsaken nor his seed begging for bread."

As Avery turned and closed the door, he was a bit surprised to see that there was a stricken look on the face of his employer.

Mr. Jenkins sighed, "I have no verses to quote, but Avery Brown is one of the best men I ever met."

Avery's steps were slow as he returned to the house. When he walked in, he could see that Mae was surprised he had returned so quickly. She obviously thought that he and Mr. Jenkins would be awhile in working out the terms of a new contract.

"Well, Mae," he looked at his faithful wife, whom he loved more than he could ever tell her. He paused, finding the words difficult to say. "I guess we had better start packing. I just lost my job!"

CHAPTER 12

Another Move

ELLA MAE LOOKED around at the pile of boxes and the odds and ends of furniture the men had brought into the house and deposited wherever they found a spot. The small cottage Avery had rented for them barely contained their furniture. There were three bedrooms in this bungalow-type house; one for Granny, one for them, and one for Mary Lou and Jo Angeline, which meant Ben would have to sleep in the living room. Again, it seemed that it would be a bleak Christmas.

Mae was a little ashamed of herself for feeling this way. Christ was still on His throne, and He certainly was worthy of being worshipped and celebrated, even in the midst of dismal circumstances. After seeking forgiveness, Mae began to think about all of their blessings. They had a place to live, were warm, and had food to eat.

With that thought, Mae's mind flew to the goose a friend had brought them for dinner. A good laugh dispelled any hint of dissatisfaction that was in the air. What a time she and Granny had experienced trying to pick the feathers from that goose! She had picked the feathers from many, many chickens. So she thought that surely they could do the same with one small goose. The strong outer feathers were not too hard to pull off, but the soft down resisted the scalding water, and it was almost impossible to pull it away from the dry skin. They originally had thoughts of keeping the downy feathers to stuff a pillow, but the more they tried to capture the soft, light feathers, the more they floated away from their grabbing fingers.

It ended up that Ella Mae had to skin the goose before she could dress it and put it in the oven to bake. Days later, they still were finding soft, white feathers clinging to the ceiling or furniture, even to their clothing.

Glad for the relief that laughter brought to her discouraged thoughts, Mae continued naming her blessings. She talked out loud to Granny as she enumerated them.

At least Ben did not have to change schools. And Mary Lou would now attend the same school as Ben and ride the bus with him. Mae thought that the young girl secretly was pleased and felt quite grown up, even if she seemed a little nervous at first.

This was the first time Ella Mae had been glad that her family had diminished in size. What would she have done with one more person to make a space for?

At this new home, there was nothing for Mae to do outside and nothing to do inside except cook and keep the house as straight as possible. She always had wanted more time to crochet, but now that she had the time, the joy of doing it almost had disappeared. There was no space to use her sewing machine, so that meant no quilting, no making of new dresses for Mary Lou, and no mending except what she could do by hand. How in the world did the women who could not sew or garden or raise chickens spend their time?

In late February, Avery came in and told Mae that he had secured a job with a Mr. Randolph, owner of a large farm, and that he would begin work on the first day of March. Mae was so relieved that she could have cried. Although he had not complained about being out of work, she knew how humiliated Avery felt. A friend had hired him as a carpenter's helper, and the money was welcome, but he was a farmer, and there was nothing like the feel of good earth under his feet and the touch of a cow under his hand.

As soon as Mr. Randolph and he had agreed upon the terms of his employment, Avery took Mae to see the house. She was pleased at the pretty cottage and the way it sat at the top of a sloping hill, far from the highway. She took careful note of the inside of the house and the way it was laid out so that when moving day came, she would know where to place their furniture.

In addition to the two bedrooms upstairs, there were two downstairs, plus a nice living room with a fireplace, a large dining room, and a kitchen with a pump right outside the door. A wide front porch covered the front of the house and a smaller porch extended from the kitchen. If there was any disappointment at all about the house, it was the lack of indoor plumbing. Since they had never had that luxury, she reckoned they could do without it awhile longer. She hoped that someday they would enjoy that modern convenience.

Mae could see that Granny was rapidly getting to the place where she was going to need extra care and chose one of the downstairs rooms for her. It would be less work, and she could hear her call if there was a need.

Avery also noted that Granny was very tired, and they put her bed together first. Mae proceeded to smooth out the featherbed and put clean linens in place. As soon as she was finished, Mae urged her mother to lie down and rest until dinner was ready. It did not take much coaxing.

Mae could tell the men were making good headway with the furniture, so she tackled the kitchen. Avery had started a fire in the kitchen stove, and the kitchen was already cozy. Mae had been a little sad at leaving her old kitchen range behind, but the house they'd rented had a gas stove in the kitchen, and this house had an almost new wood range from Montgomery Ward. It had a water tank on one side, next to the firebox, and a spigot at the bottom. There would be warm water as long as there was a fire in the stove.

She still kept her cast iron teakettles on the back of the stove. She figured that a person could never have too much hot water. Like her old stove, this one had two warming ovens over the top of the stove so that heat from the stove top would keep whatever was placed inside warm until it was removed.

Mae had packed a good dinner for them before they left their rented house that morning. All she needed to do right now was make the coffee. It did not take long for the water to start perking, and the smell of hot coffee brought the men to the door, ready to eat. Mae showed them where the wash basin was and the clean towels. Soon all was ready.

Her head had been aching since early morning and was getting steadily worse, but there was no time to do anything about that except take an aspirin or two and keep working. They would have to hustle to get the beds put together and in place if they were to have a place to sleep tonight.

Mr. Randolph came that afternoon and met the family. He explained to Ben about the school bus. He would have to walk to the end of the long lane, which wound around the barn and down the hill, over the little bridge at the bottom, and up the next hill, perhaps a good half mile, to catch the bus each morning. Avery would have to pay ten cents a day for him to ride. Mary Lou would walk to the two room school she would attend.

Avery had been very careful in working out all the conditions of his employment before moving. He was to receive forty dollars a month, plus ten dollars for Ben to help with the milking, morning and evening. He could have a week's vacation each summer, provided he had someone to take care of the milking while he was away.

Avery also was to have his own Jersey cow. The black and white Holstein cows were pretty and gave a lot of milk, but the fat content of the milk was very low. Avery knew that Mae liked good cream for use in cooking and for making the golden butter she liked to churn. He liked rich cream for his coffee.

He was responsible for the milking, but the work of the dairy was done by two ladies. Both had worked for Mr. Randolph for several years. They kept everything sparkling clean and helped with the milking as needed. There were other tenants who took care of other herds and helped with the crops. Altogether, it sounded like a good situation for Avery.

There was a good chicken house, and Avery could raise his own hogs. Any pigs that were born to these hogs were his to sell or butcher for food. Mae was delighted with the chicken house. Ben helped her clean it and put fresh straw in the nests and on the floor. It happened that the man who rented Avery the house they lived in while he looked for work owned a poultry farm. A trip back to his place resulted in a dozen laying hens and a rooster, plus two setting hens with three dozen eggs. Setting hens were ones who no longer laid eggs but refused to leave their nests. They wanted to sit on a clutch of eggs, usually as many as their wings could cover.

Mae placed eight brown eggs under each setting hen. The remaining eggs would be for breakfast, until the other hens settled down and began to lay eggs. By the time the new chickens hatched, there would be a steady supply of eggs for eating and cooking.

While Mae worked at setting the house in order, Avery went to the nearest store for items Mae needed. He established credit with the local merchant. The store was located at a crossroads, and another grocery store was on the opposite corner. Their prices differed on one or two items, but generally, they were about the same. One merchant was hesitant about extending credit and only allowed a set amount and a limited time for payment. The other one had always had good relations with the men who worked for Mr. Randolph and made an agreement with Avery for his shopping needs.

The children quickly settled into school, and life fell into a familiar pattern. Avery liked the farm and was much relieved to find the other workers friendly and with much the same work ethic as his own.

Sunday morning found them at the nearest Baptist church. As before, much of the congregation was originally from the south, and they were glad to welcome the new family into their midst. Several invitations to Sunday dinner were extended, some more emphatic than others. Since there were boys and girls of matching ages at one of the homes, the Wells', this was the one they accepted. Thus began a lifelong friendship and habit of exchanging visits from one house to the other.

In the years to come, Avery and Ella Mae often visited back and forth with the Wells family. Avery was as fond of Mr. Wells as Mae was of Mrs. Wells. Although, they thought it unusual that this couple never called each other by their given names. It was always Mr. and Mrs. Wells. For the lifetime of their friendship, that never changed.

As the Brown family got to know more and more people at their new church, they found that most of the families that attended the small church they joined were related to each other. It took a little getting used to for the Browns to figure out which children belonged to which family, as all the cousins and their parents visited back and forth. There was little need for discipline, as the children knew that Mama and Papa would hear of their behavior from someone and possibly from more than one person.

For the first time in the last few months, Avery and Ella Mae could relax and enjoy their life. Truly this did begin to feel like the "promised land."

CHAPTER 13

A Chapter Closes

*S*PRING CAME AND went, and summer's heat and humidity soon would arrive. Gardening was done, and vegetables were beginning to ripen. There was a sense of rivalry among the women at the church. They all were waiting to see who would have the first ripe tomatoes and first mess of green beans to eat. They would share these at the Sunday dinners that often were eaten under shade trees on tables made from planks thrown across sawhorses. Sheets served as tablecloths and could be put in the laundry when the meal was finished.

Granny seemed content in her new surroundings, but Mae noticed that she spent more and more time in her room. She hardly talked at all, and in spite of Avery's attempts to tease her, she did not respond as usual. Sometimes she looked at him or at one of the children as if she did not quite know who they were. When she did talk, it was as if they were still living in Grassy Creek. Mae watched her closely when she went outside for her daily walk and advised the children to keep an eye on her, as she sometimes got confused about where she was going.

One afternoon, Mary Lou caught a glimpse of Granny walking down the lane on the other side of the barn. She ran in to tell her mother.

"Go after her and tell her to come back," Mae instructed. "You may have to take her by the hand, but be kind."

Mary Lou obviously did not feel kind. She was aggravated. Mae knew she felt she had better things to do than chase after Granny.

As Mary Lou hurried out of the house, she muttered, "Why does she have to be so contrary?"

Mae kept her eyes out as she watched Mary Lou run after her grandmother.

When she reached her, Mary Lou told Granny to come back to the house, but she kept on walking.

"Come on, Granny! You are going the wrong way! Momma wants you to come back to the house."

"Let me be, child. I am going to visit Annie, and I'm late already."

"No, Granny, Annie doesn't live there. You have to come home with me. Momma's waiting." Mary Lou took her hand, but Granny simply shook it off and started on again.

Mary Lou ran back to the house and reported her efforts and what had happened. "Momma, I can't get her to come. I tried to make her, but she won't stop. You'll have to come, Momma!"

Mae was in the middle of rolling out the crust for pies for supper, but she could see that Granny would soon be out of sight. Mary Lou was out of breath, and it was useless to send her out again. Of course, Ben was not anywhere within calling distance, so she quickly washed her hands and started out after her mother. She rounded the barn and saw that Granny was quite a ways down the lane, so Mae quickened her steps.

When she finally caught up with her mother, Granny was confused and could not understand what all the commotion was about. However, she meekly followed Mae back to the house. That was the last time she ventured out of her bedroom.

Granny continued to decline, and by the beginning of fall was not getting out of bed at all. Mae carried her food to her and eventually ended up feeding her. Some days Granny recognized her, but most days, she did not seem to know who anyone was or where she was.

Eileen wrote to tell her parents that Garvin was not feeling well. He had not been able to go to work for several days and almost had passed out in class one day. She had sent for a doctor, but he did not seem to know what was wrong and had just advised bed rest.

Avery was making arrangements to go to the city and see for himself what needed to be done to get Garvin on his feet again. But before he could get ready, Uncle Carl came, bringing Garvin and his luggage home.

Mae went to the door and saw Uncle Carl helping Garvin out of the car. Avery hurried down the steps, and the two men helped Garvin into the house and onto a chair. Uncle Carl left to call the doctor and returned to tell the worried parents that Dr. Harvey was on his way.

While they waited for the doctor to arrive, Ella Mae put Garvin in her bed. She never had seen him so pale. She tried to talk to him, but that seemed to be beyond Garvin's strength at the moment. She placed her hand on his forehead and brushed his hair back. Prayers fled upward as she fought the tears that wanted to flow. She knew her son was already afraid, and seeing her fear would not help him. So she prayed the harder and stayed by his side until she heard the doctor step into the house.

It had not been necessary for them to have the services of a doctor in the three years they had lived in Maryland. The kind face and warm handshake as Dr. Harvey introduced himself brought a measure of confidence to Mae as she led him into the bedroom, where an exhausted Garvin waited.

Mae, Avery, and Uncle Carl stood silently by while Garvin was examined. He answered the doctor's questions as well as he could, and the effort seemed to take all of his strength. Ben and Mary Lou sat quietly in the living room. They did not understand what was going on and strained to hear what the doctor might say. It was a long time before the grownups came out of the bedroom.

Dr. Harvey sat down at the table, and everyone gathered around to hear what he had to say. Mary Lou stood by her mother's chair, and Ben pulled his chair close on the other side. Avery pulled Mary Lou up onto his lap, and Mae put a comforting arm around Ben. They all were anxious to learn what Dr. Harvey had to tell them--anxious and afraid at the same time.

"Well, folks, Garvin seems to have all the signs of rheumatic fever. This is a disease that usually happens to children but sometimes can occur in young adults. It usually develops two or three weeks after a person has strep throat or scarlet fever. Sometimes it may take up to five weeks to show up. Do you know if he has had either of these diseases?"

Mae thought for a moment. "I believe he did have a very bad cold a few weeks ago. He never said much about it, so we thought he was over it. What is rheumatic fever, and how can you tell that's what it is?"

"Rheumatic fever is an inflammatory disease that can involve the heart, joints, skin, and brain. It most usually develops in people who have an untreated strep infection. It gets its name from the similarity to rheumatism. Do you know if your son saw a doctor about his cold?"

"I doubt it," Avery replied. "He probably thought it was just a cold and likely did not have the money for a doctor."

"Yes, well, 'just a cold' can turn into a lot of other things. What we have to deal with here is heart complications, I believe. This can lead to serious damage to the heart valves, if left untreated."

"What do we need to do? I don't have much money, but I can borrow some, if it is necessary."

"Let's not worry about the money right now," the kind doctor obviously had been practicing medicine in this area for several years now and was well acquainted with the financial standing of most tenant farmers. "What this boy must have, if he is to survive at all, is plenty of bed rest. It may take as much as a year of intense rest. I don't mean just a nap in the afternoon. I'm talking about complete bed rest. Do you think you can manage that?"

"Yes," Mae answered. "Of course, we will manage. What are the consequences of this disease?"

"The leg joints can become inflamed and very painful. Congestive heart failure with shortness of breath and the development of a heart murmur is another result. A long-lasting rash that gets worse with heat and a flailing of arms and legs can occur unless treatment is begun immediately. It is not a pleasant disease. I am going to write you a prescription for what medicine is available, and you must give it to him exactly as prescribed. It does not taste pleasant, but that's not important. Also, he will need iron tablets every day, and I suggest you feed him liver at least twice a week. Calf liver is the best, but unfortunately, it is the most expensive. I'm going to leave you some pills that I want you to begin immediately, and I would like to visit him at least once a week until we see how things are going. Would that be satisfactory with you?"

Avery and Ella Mae both agreed and assured the doctor they would follow his instructions.

Dr. Harvey looked at Ben and Mary Lou. He patted Mary Lou on the head and looked Ben in the eye. "Your mother is going to need some help with all of this extra work. Do you think you are big enough to help her out?"

Both children instantly agreed.

As soon as the doctor was gone, Uncle Carl helped Avery bring the furniture from the living room into the dining room. Then they brought one of the beds down from upstairs. Ben carried the bedclothes down, and Mary Lou carried the pillow. When it was all ready, they helped Garvin make the journey to his new resting place.

"This will make it easy for me to take care of you. This way you won't be shut away in a separate room from the family. Also, when people come to visit, you will be right there. It will soon be cool enough for a fire in the fireplace, and just think how cozy that will be." Ella Mae spoke as if this were her idea all along. Garvin looked at her, but didn't seem to care. He quickly went to sleep.

The summer progressed and settled into a pattern. Granny did not improve, and toward the end of October, slipped into a coma. She did not respond to Ella Mae or to Avery at all.

Dr. Harvey came early one morning and checked her. He did not suggest taking her to the hospital or performing any kind of measure to revive her. Death was sometimes a welcome visitor. He looked in on Garvin, and on his way to the car, he suggested to Avery that he stay close to the house that day. In his opinion, the end was very near, and he thought Avery should be the one who sat with Granny that morning.

Ella Mae did not fear death. She knew the time was near for her mother to leave this life for another. She had said her good-byes to Granny days ago and already had grieved the loss of her mother. But she was grateful when Uncle Carl came and entered the room with Avery.

It was Saturday, and the children were home from school. Ella Mae cleared off the breakfast dishes. Mary

Lou had come over to stand beside her mother, when Mae suddenly realized she had not eaten anything that morning. She fixed herself a plate of biscuits and gravy and poured herself the last of the coffee.

Mae put her arm around her daughter. "Why don't you go in and see how Granny is doing? Be real quiet and don't try to talk to her."

Mary Lou did as she was told. She had not liked to go into Granny's room since she became ill. She quietly opened the door and saw Daddy take Granny's hand and put it under the sheet. Then he pulled the sheet over Granny's face.

Daddy looked at Mary Lou but said nothing.

Uncle Carl said, "Mary Lou, go tell your mother that it's over. Granny is gone."

Mary Lou wanted to ask some questions but did as she was told. She returned to the table and said, "She's gone."

Ella Mae put down her fork and folded her napkin. Mary Lou did not know what to say or do, so she simply waited. She thought her mother should cry or say something. She certainly would cry if her mother died. She was not old enough to understand that being a caregiver for a long period of time had a way of drying up one's tears.

Uncle Carl soon left to "make arrangements," and Daddy took Mother into the kitchen, where they talked in low tones. Mary Lou knew this was not the time to ask for explanations. So she found Ben, and the two of them spent the morning trying to keep busy and out of the way.

Granny was to be buried in North Carolina. That meant her body would have to be taken back by train. Ella Mae felt she could not leave Garvin, and as much as she would have liked to attend her mother's funeral, Avery was the one who was going to go.

The funeral was not the only thing Avery and Mae had talked about in the kitchen. Avery had felt for some time that they probably would never return to the little farm in North Carolina. He had already confided to Carl that he might need to sell the farm while he was there for Granny's funeral.

"Now, Avery," Uncle Carl had put a hand on Avery's arm. "You had better be very sure. Don't do anything until you can talk it over with Ella Mae. You know how she loved that little place. Let's not be in too big of a hurry about this."

But Avery could not see wasting the trip when he believed they would have to sell the farm sooner or later. For his part, he liked the opportunities he saw in Maryland. He did, however, carefully broach the subject with Ella Mae. He knew full well how Mae loved their little home and that in one sense she would always regret leaving it.

Mae, on the other hand, realized the financial strain Avery was laboring under. There was the extra expense of the funeral and burial, and who knew how long Garvin would need special medicine and maybe extra care. It was true that her home in North Carolina always would have a special place in her heart. She often missed the quietness of the hills, but she knew God was present here. The rolling hills of Maryland might not be as steep as those in North Carolina, but God is the same wherever His children live. Mae knew from experience that life is what you make of it, and her children certainly had more opportunities here than they did in the small community of Grassy Creek. Besides, she realized many of her one-time friends had moved away and going "home" was no longer the same.

When Avery approached her about the possibility of selling the farm while he was there for Granny's funeral, Mae only asked him the one question she always asked when important decisions were to be made: "Have you prayed about this, Avery?"

Avery pulled his wife into his arms, and for the first time, she let the tears fall until his shirt was wet. "Yes, Mae. I've prayed about it, and while I see it as the best thing to do, if you still think you want to go back some day, we will hold onto it for awhile longer."

"Go ahead and sell it, then."

He pulled his handkerchief from his pocket and wiped her eyes. Then with a quick kiss, he started out of the door.

"Avery, just one more thing. Make sure we can go back and get Mother's three-cornered cupboard out of the dining room. I want Riley to have that."

Avery nodded and quickly left before Mae could change her mind.

Before Avery left for North Carolina, members from the church attended the brief funeral service that was held at the house. As soon as the service ended, the funeral director took the casket and Avery to the train station. Eileen and Riley came home for the funeral and took charge of serving sandwiches, cake, and coffee to the people who stayed for a few minutes with Ella Mae.

The house was strangely quiet after the door closed and Ella Mae heard the last car pull out of the driveway. Riley took Dad's car and drove Eileen back to her apartment. She needed to be at work the next day, if at all possible. Mae saw that Ben and Mary Lou were off to bed, tended to Garvin's needs, and then went to bed herself.

Sleep did not come immediately. Bible verses and a storehouse of memories flooded her soul. She was going to miss her mother. True, Granny and Avery had their differences, but what did that matter? Life had a way of sorting out what was important and what needed to be left behind. Mother had helped as long as she was able, and her love for Ella Mae had been a solid rock in Mae's life. She was glad they had given Granny a home.

Mae was at peace as her heart followed the path of her mother back to the hills she loved. It gave her comfort to know that her mother was at home and that one day, she would greet her mother again.

CHAPTER 14

Life Continues

*L*IFE RETURNED TO a more normal pattern. The dog days of summer were upon them again. The last of the garden was done, except for the making of chow-chow out of the remnants of the late vegetables. This relish would taste good in the coming winter as a compliment to whatever they had for supper. Although Ella Mae continued to have a persistent headache, she excused it as something that came from the stress of the past few months.

Mae liked the moment of quiet at the end of each day. She made an effort to get the children all bathed and their hair combed before Avery came in for supper. It helped calm everyone down and gave her a moment to catch her breath before it was time to put the food on the table. The drowsiness of the afternoon seemed to invade her very being.

One evening, after Jo had been really fussy all day and Avery had reprimanded her pretty harshly at dinnertime, Ella Mae pulled her up on her lap to comb out her curls. She loved the blonde curls that lay in ringlets all over Jo's head. Mae brushed her hand over the child's head and immediately was alarmed at how warm Jo felt. She asked Ben to bring her a basin of warm water so that she could bath her off a little.

Before Ben could obey, Jo stiffened out, and her eyes rolled back in her head. White with alarm, Ella Mae ordered Ben to run to the barn and get Avery. "Hurry, Ben!"

Her order to hurry was not needed, for Ben could see that something was dreadfully wrong with his little sister. Mae was sure he was worried that his sister was dead.

Ben ran as fast as he could, and although it was not that far to the barn, it seemed like he would never get there. Avery came equally as fast and took one look at his baby before running to get the car. He drove as fast as the car would go to Mr. Randolph's house to use the telephone to call Dr. Harvey. Then he drove as fast as he dared back to the house.

Ella Mae laid Jo on their bed, but she showed no sign of movement. Avery fell to his knees and cried out their plea for God to be merciful to their little girl. Ella Mae continued to bath the child's hot face with the washcloth. It seemed hours before they heard the sound of Dr. Harvey's car as he pulled into the driveway.

After a careful examination, Dr. Harvey turned to the anxious parents. "I don't want to scare you, but we have a very sick little girl on our hands. I believe we have a case of acute nephritis, which is a failure of the kidneys to function properly. We'll talk more about it, but right now, our problem is to revive her. She is in a crisis state right now. You have been doing the right thing by trying to cool her down. I'm going to stay until her fever breaks."

Avery left the room. He needed to be where he could cry out to the Lord for mercy and for forgiveness for the way he had been cross with Jo. He hurried to the dairy with a heart that felt like it would burst. He chipped off a basin of ice from the box where the milk was stored to keep it cool until the truck came to pick it up in the morning.

Avery knew that the ladies who worked in the dairy saw the tears running down his face. They had never been too friendly with Mr. Brown, as they called him, but trouble comes to everyone at some time in his or her life, and they had heard the message Ben had brought to the barn for him. He saw the concern on their faces and knew they liked his pretty little girl with the golden curls and did not like the thought of any child having to suffer.

"Mr. Brown," one of the sisters said, "we'll finish up here. Don't worry about the work. We have done it by ourselves before. Just go ahead and help Mrs. Brown take care of the little girl."

Avery nodded, too full of worry to answer. He determined to be more mindful of these women in the days ahead. "God bless you," he mumbled.

The sisters didn't know about that. They were not on a talking level with the Lord. Most of the so-called Christians they knew looked down at them because of the kind of work they did. Milking and all the chores connected with it were considered man's work. But if Mr. Brown wanted God to bless them, they said they reckoned it would not hurt.

Avery hurried to the house and took the basin of tepid water from Ella Mae, dropping in chunks of ice to cool it down. There had been no change in Jo's status in the few minutes he had been gone. He motioned for Ella Mae to change places with him, and he took over her task of keeping the cold washcloths on Jo's forehead. As soon as one began to feel warm, he exchanged it for a cold one. He knelt beside the bed, praying with all his heart for Jo to wake up. He tried to reason with God, he bargained with Him—anything to have the power of the Almighty help his little girl.

Ella Mae was on her knees on the other side of the bed, joining her prayers with those of her husband. God had promised that where two or three where gathered, He would be with them. She knew the heavenly Father was with them, but she wanted more. She wanted Him to do something. She remembered to pray that God's will would be done. But she prayed with all the earnestness of her heart that His will would be to make her little girl well.

"Please, dear God," she found she was not above trying to trade promises for help. "I'll do whatever You ask. Please don't take her from us."

Two frightened children hovered near the door, watching. Ben and Mary Lou did not bother to remind Mother that it was suppertime. Even after darkness descended, they did not say they were hungry. There would be time enough to eat when Jo woke up and could join them. Ben did not even tease Mary Lou as he usually did.

They finally decided they should say some prayers so that Mother and Daddy would not have to do it all. The two of them knelt by the couch and asked their heavenly Father to please let Jo get well. They found a book, and even though they tried to stay awake until Jo woke up, their eyes grew heavier and heavier and soon closed completely.

Dr. Harvey checked Jo's pulse again. He thought that maybe he should go home and get some rest. It had been a long day, making house calls from one end of the county to the other. He had lots of poor families in his care, and most of them were hard workers. But this little family had somehow found a way into his heart. He had watched the way Ella Mae accepted the extra work of caring for her son when she already was burdened with the care of an invalid mother. There was never any question about whether or not she would be able to do it.

He also had been aware of the headaches Mae kept having. No matter how often he mentioned coming into the office for an examination, she always made some excuse. His suspicion was that she did not want to add one ounce of worry or one cent of expense to their already stretched resources. No, he would wait until he knew the outcome of this new situation. He had been known to add a prayer or two of his own when he had reached the end of his knowledge and abilities.

Time moves slowly when hearts are heavy. Midnight came and went with no sign of change. Ella Mae checked on the children but found them fast asleep and decided to leave them alone for the present. She made coffee and offered some ham and biscuits to Avery and Dr. Harvey. Avery could not eat anything, but Dr. Harvey welcomed the respite.

Dr. Harvey just had finished his coffee when he saw Jo move. He was by her side instantly and kept his hand on her pulse as she slowly opened her eyes.

Jo woke up and started to sit up in the bed. "Why are Momma and Daddy crying? Why do I have to lay down again?"

An abundance of joy and praising the Lord went on for several minutes. Dr. Harvey examined his patient and was soon satisfied that her fever indeed had broken and she was on her way to recovery. He talked to her and to Avery and Ella Mae for a few more minutes and then bade them a weary "good night" as he packed up his bag and went quietly out the door.

Were the stars really a little brighter, or was it merely that he was looking at them through the mist gathered in his eyes? He did not try to analyze the sudden way Jo's fever had broken or what really had happened in that bedroom. He was just grateful.

A shooting star drew his attention again to the sky. A Bible verse he had learned as a child in Sunday school came to mind. "The heavens declare the glory of God and the firmament showeth his handiwork." Dr. Harvey paused. "Your healing power shows Your handiwork, too, Lord. I thank You. And I'm sure You will accept the thanks of an old Methodist for having an old Baptist bring my attention back to faith in all Your works. I needed Your help this night, and I thank You for it."

CHAPTER 15

Ella Mae

AVERY SLIPPED QUIETLY in at the kitchen door. He had been worried about Mae all day. She had not been her usual cheerful self. True, she certainly was tired after all the work she had done over the past few months. The nursing of Granny and Garvin would have been too much for most women. Avery had wanted to call Eileen to take a leave of absence and return home to help her mother, but Mae would not hear of it. She worried that Eileen might lose her job since she had just gotten started. He did make sure that Ben and Mary Lou did all the little things they were big enough to do. They were a big help, but the majority of the work still fell on his wife.

It was Christmas time again, with the usual flurry of decorating and making sure there were special things for dinner. Eileen came home with huge armloads of gifts. Riley came from school for the holiday, making the family complete, except for those far away.

Christmas Eve found them all at church, where the children had recitations to say and special songs to sing. Ben was successful in getting out of having to recite this year. Ella Mae agreed that perhaps he was too old.

Following the pageant of the birth of the Christ Child and the visit of the Magi, all the lights were turned out. Each member of the congregation held a candle. The first one was lit by the pastor. Then light was passed from candle to candle until the room was full of their soft glow. The strains of "Silent Night" sounded out into the night as the people filed out, singing this most beloved carol. Once they were outside the building, the calls of "Merry Christmas" filled the air as friends and neighbors greeted one another before leaving for home.

The next morning brought happy cries of "Merry Christmas" as Mary Lou and Ben hurried to the Christmas tree to see which packages had their names on them. Happily, there were several. Avery was grateful that the children voted to wait until the boys and he came in from milking to open their gifts.

Everyone was excited about their presents. A new game called "Monopoly" provided hours of pleasure for the boys, and even Mary Lou was taught how to play. Garvin would sometimes plead weariness if he was losing, and that earned him the name "poor loser."

They all had learned early not to argue over a game. Daddy's rule was: "If you can't play without fighting, you can't play."

Mary Lou received a new set of books, *Nancy Drew, Student Nurse*, which kept her happy until she had read them all. Then she began to peruse them again, with more attention this time. Daddy got a new overcoat, and Mother a new dress. Eileen, Garvin, and Riley were not left out. The contents of each of their boxes were looked at and examined over and over as they all talked and laughed together.

When all the gifts had been opened, Eileen said, "I'm hongry!"

Everyone laughed, and their thoughts went back to that Christmas when they had first met Freddie.

Mae and Eileen went to the kitchen to fix breakfast as they recalled the household of mentally challenged people that they considered poor.

"But, you know, Mother," commented Eileen, "they were happy in their own way. There was love in that home, except perhaps for Freddie. I wonder where he is today."

"While we are being thankful for our wonderful blessings, we will remember Freddie and others like him. At least we know God loves him, and perhaps something will be done to provide a good home for him before too much longer."

That afternoon, Mae went to lie down. It was not like her to take a nap, but Avery chalked it up to the big dinner and the reaction to all the stress of getting ready for Christmas.

When he went into the bedroom to tell Mae he was leaving for the barn, he was surprised to see that she had a damp cloth over her forehead. "What's the matter, Mae?"

Mae struggled to sit up. "Oh, that headache is back again. It was pretty bad this time, but I'll be okay as soon as I take an aspirin."

"Why don't you stay in bed awhile longer? We can eat leftovers for supper."

"I'll be fine. Mary Lou can help get supper on the table."

Avery called Ben to go with him to do the evening milking. He thought that Mae had been taking a lot of aspirin lately. Maybe he had better pay more attention to how she was feeling. A visit to Dr. Harvey might be in order.

Mae was up and about when Ben and he came in for dinner. Avery figured that maybe a good night's sleep was all she needed.

At nine o'clock he turned on the evening news and listened to Lowell Thomas talk about what was going on in the world. Everyone knew it was time for bed when the newscast was over. All in all it had been a happy day.

After Christmas, Eileen returned to her job, and life took on its regular pattern. Garvin was rapidly improving. In fact, Dr. Harvey felt that if Garvin continued to improve, he would be able to return to school by Easter. This proved to be the case, and even though Ella Mae worried that he might have a relapse, she agreed that the thought of getting back to normal living was the very medicine he needed right now.

Mae's headaches continued. In addition, her eyesight steadily had begun to fail, until she hardly could see across the room. She became convinced that she was going blind but did not mention her fear to anyone. Instead, as soon as everyone was out of the house for the morning, she began a practice of counting her steps from the stove to the table, from the table to the door, and then to all the other places she traveled during the day. She also practiced moving pots and pans around on the stove with her eyes closed.

She knew that one day soon she must tell Avery. But she also was aware that money was tight, and the first thing Avery would want to do would be to take her to the doctor. She prayed continually that God would allow her to keep her sight, at least until Ben was out of school and Mary Lou was a little older to help with the housework.

Mae did not hear Avery turn the doorknob and quietly enter the kitchen. He stood still and watched as she walked from place to place, counting as she walked. When she suddenly stopped and held her head as she began to cry, he was at her side, perplexed and scared. What was happening to his wife?

Through tears, Mae finally told Avery all about her increasing headaches and her failing eyesight.

Avery held her and reminded her of the promise that God had given that He always would be with her and that "when you pass through the waters they shall not overtake thee." Then, without another word, Avery bundled her into the car and headed for Dr. Harvey's office. He did not scold Mae for not telling him about her problem because he had lived with her long enough to know how she thought.

They did not have an appointment, and Dr. Harvey's office was filled with patients in various stages of needing his care. But when he looked out his office window and saw Avery helping Ella Mae out of the car, he told his nurse to open the back door and bring them directly to him. He finished with the lady he was examining, and as soon as the door closed behind her, he motioned for Avery to bring Ella Mae in.

Dr. Harvey listened to Mae's story and began his examination of her head. The more he discovered, the more dismayed he became. First, he berated himself for not insisting on her coming in when she first mentioned that she was having headaches. He could not imagine how much pain she had endured, all because she did not want to worry her husband or cause him to spend money on her.

"Well, it looks like a bad case of infected sinuses. I only hope you have not waited too long to save your eyesight. You must go to the hospital as soon as I can get you in. Avery, you will need to get someone to drive you to Johns Hopkins as soon as I can make arrangements. We'll contact the doctor. I have a friend who specializes in this kind of case. By the time you get there, a bed will be ready for her."

Ella Mae started to object, but Dr. Harvey simply held up his hand. "No arguments allowed. This is something that cannot wait. Avery, hire someone to take over at home for about a week, maybe two. If you want your wife to keep even a part of her eyesight, you must do as I say. A prayer or two on her behalf won't hurt either."

Avery asked the nurse to call Carl for him, and then he got Mae in the car to head home. The ride was quiet.

He wanted to comfort hi wife but realized that he needed help as much as she did.

"Avery…" Mae started to argue about the doctor's order to go to the hospital, but Avery shushed her quickly. She knew it was true that she needed help.

The big question that was on both of their minds as they drove was who to get to take care of Avery and the children. They also wondered where they would get the money to pay for all of this.

After the scare with Jo, Avery had decided it was high time they had a telephone. He had imposed on Mr. Randolph long enough. Mae was too weary at the time to protest, and she agreed her mind would be more at ease. Thus, as soon as they arrived home, Avery was able to call the pastor and ask for prayers for Mae.

After that, he had to return to work. But he reassured Mae that they would find someone to help with the children, and if push came to shove, he would call Eileen to come home until Mae was able to take over the work again.

Mae sat down to rest and think. She prayed that they would not need to call Eileen. Then she thought of a niece who might be able to come and immediately placed a call and told her of the need. Unfortunately, the niece just had taken another job and could not afford to give it up so soon after being hired.

Her next thought was of a lady from North Carolina who recently had moved to Maryland to be with her son. She might be glad to make a little extra money. Mae did not think the lady was as clean as she could be, but they could live with a little dirt until Mae got home from the hospital. The lady's son answered the telephone and gave his regrets to Mae. His mother had fallen and broken her hip. It would be weeks before she would be up and about. Mae thanked him and hung up.

Mae took her burden to the Lord. Surely He could help her find someone if she truly had to obey Dr. Harvey's orders. Mae recalled God's promise to the people of Israel that before they called, He would answer, and while they were yet speaking, He heard them and was ready to answer. She had not even finished her prayer when the phone rang.

"Hello, Ella Mae. This is Ruby Howell. I just heard that you are going to the hospital."

"Yes, I guess I have no choice." Ella Mae wondered if Ruby just called to find out the details. She was known as one who liked to be in on any news about people in the congregation.

Ruby did not keep her waiting. "Pastor Leroy suggested that you might be looking for someone to help with housekeeping until you are well again. I would like to come over and talk to you about the job, unless you already have someone."

Ella Mae scarcely could believe her ears. "When can you come? Avery will be finished milking about five-thirty. He will want to talk to you too."

Assured that Ruby would be there by that time, Ella Mae hung up the phone and fell on her knees. She wondered why she was so surprised that God had been as good as His word. She had turned to Him for help and He already had provided someone to help her. Were other Christians as surprised as she when God answered their prayers?

Ruby Howell was a fine Christian lady, a widow and well able to meet their needs. She was not a person that one easily took to. In spite of her many attributes, she was not overly friendly. Neither Avery nor the children liked her very much. However, they had to have someone, and surely she would not charge much for her service.

Promptly at five-thirty, she knocked on their door. Mae already had explained what was happening to Ben and Mary Lou. They were scared at the thought that Mother was going to the hospital, but she reassured them that there would be someone to care for them, and of course, Daddy would be there to see that all was well.

The three adults sat down to talk, and Ruby explained that she would go home each night but would return in time to get breakfast and get the children off to school. During the day, in addition to taking care of Jo, she would do the household chores, including laundry, and prepare dinner and supper before going back to her home. She asked $5.00 per day for her services. She did not work on Sundays, but she would make sure there was plenty of food prepared for the day.

Avery and Ella Mae looked at each other. That was more money than Avery made in a month, but they did not seem to have a choice. While they still were talking about what had to be done, Dr. Harvey called and told Avery to have Ella Mae at the hospital at seven o'clock the next morning. He said she probably would be there for two weeks.

Mae's heart sank. She had hoped to be gone no more than three days. Now it was going to be two weeks. Would Avery be able to keep everything on an even keel while she was gone? She would have to trust him and trust the Lord to keep it so.

The next morning, Ruby drove into the yard in plenty of time to receive last minute instructions as to what needed to be done. Ben and Mary Lou wasted no time in getting ready for school. Mrs. Howell let them know that she expected their beds to be made and everything put in order before they left the house. She packed their lunches of peanut butter and honey and prepared to send them off, quietly commenting that she might have her hands full for the next two weeks; although they had given her no reason for such thoughts.

Uncle Carl came right on time to drive Avery and Mae to Johns Hopkins. Avery drove well enough on the county roads, but he was not confident enough to attempt driving in a city as big as Baltimore. Before she left, Mae kissed Jo, Ben, and Mary Lou good-bye and urged them to be good for Mrs. Howell while she was gone.

Uncle Carl and Avery stayed at the hospital that day until Mae's examination was completed and surgery scheduled for the following morning. Avery had to be home in time to milk, although the sisters who worked in the dairy had assured him they would handle the milking if he needed to stay with Ella Mae.

Avery arrived home to two worried children and a curious housekeeper. The report that their mother was going to have surgery caused a lot of anxiety for the young ones.

Mrs. Howell was a very matter-of-fact person. So she instructed the children to sit down and bow their heads. Then she said a prayer that Mother would come through the surgery just fine and soon be well and back home. She thanked the Lord for doctors and nurses who cared for the sick and knew just what to do and asked that He take care of them all while Mother was away. That settled the matter as far as Mrs. Howell was concerned.

148

But Mary Lou felt differently. Later that night, she approached her father. "Daddy, what is a sinus?"

"Well, Mary Lou, I don't know a lot about it, but it has to do with your breathing. I am going to see Dr. Harvey tomorrow, and he will explain everything to me. Tomorrow is Saturday, and you don't have to go to school. How would you and Ben like to go to the hospital with me? I don't think you will get to see your Mother because she won't be feeling very well, but you can wait in the lobby for me. Mrs. Howell can take care of Jo for one day."

The next day, Uncle Carl, Avery, and the children entered the red brick building. Ben and Mary Lou thought it looked huge. They entered the lobby, and Daddy found seats at the side of a tall, white marble statue of Christ with His arms outstretched. Mary Lou recognized Him right away. She had a picture of the same statue in her Sunday school booklet. At first she was a little afraid when Daddy and Uncle Carl walked down a long hall and left them alone. She kept looking at the face of the statue, and it seemed that He was holding out His arms to her and anyone who was hurting or afraid. It reminded her of the story her Sunday school teacher had read to them about Jesus welcoming the little children and inviting them to come to Him.

Mary Lou was surprised to see Dr. Harvey come into the lobby when the big front door opened. He saw the children right away and came over to sit down beside them.

"Well, this is an awfully big room for you to be waiting in. I bet I know who you came to see," he smiled at them.

"Daddy said we could not see her today, that children are not allowed." Mary Lou was hoping Dr. Harvey would take them with him. It *was* a big room.

"Well, that's true, but if you would like to come with me, I will take you to a waiting room closer to her. Then Daddy can come out and talk to you."

The children lost no time in following Dr. Harvey down the hall. When they came to the elevators, Dr. Harvey took Mary Lou's hand. She had never ridden in an elevator and never even seen one before. The sudden upward movement made her stomach feel funny. One look at Ben told her he was scared as well. She was glad when the elevator stopped.

Dr. Harvey took them to a nice room with a couch and several soft chairs, and then he left to check on their mother. He promised to come back and tell them how she was doing.

Mary Lou's curiosity got the better of her, and when he returned and told them Mother had undergone a sinus operation and still was asleep, she asked him her questions.

"Dr. Harvey, what is a sinus?"

Dr. Harvey sat down and took a pad and pencil and began to sketch a picture of a skull. He drew small circles behind the forehead, nose, cheeks, and eyes. "These little spaces are filled with air and have openings to the nose so you can breathe. They sometimes fill with liquid, and that's why you have to blow your nose. Unless you do that, your nose gets all stopped up, like when you have a cold, and your voice sounds like this." Dr. Harvey held his nose and tried to talk.

The children laughed with him, then tried to talk while holding their own noses.

"Why is Mommy getting her sinus operated on?" Mary Lou wanted to know.

"Well, sometimes your sinuses don't work like they should, and that means trouble—usually a headache. In your mother's case, her sinuses became so swollen that she had very bad headaches because no air could get into these little pouches to the opening of her nose. Then the pouches got infected, and that was very painful for her."

"Is she going to die?" Mary Lou asked.

Ben poked her in the ribs. "Don't say that! She's going to be better. Daddy said." He looked at Dr. Harvey for confirmation.

"Your mother is very sick. That's why she is here. There are doctors here that know all about infections and sinus problems, and they can give her better care than I could. Now I know your mother has taught you to pray, and this is what we must do. Ask God to help her get better. And while she is away from home, you have to be extra good so she will not have to worry about you. You must play with Jo because she misses her mother just like you do, and she's too little to understand why Mother is not at home."

Mary Lou nodded. "We'll be good. Won't we, Ben?"

Ben nodded his head.

Mary Lou knew he would do anything, as long as it would help their mother get well. Ben swallowed a few times and turned his head aside. He probably didn't want Dr. Harvey to see the moisture in his eyes.

Dr. Harvey explained that he was going in to check on their mother again and said he would tell them if he found out anything new.

It seemed a long time before the door opened and Daddy and Uncle Carl came in with Dr. Harvey. All three of the men sat down and began to talk. Ben and Mary Lou were very quiet. Daddy took out his handkerchief and blew his nose. Mary Lou thought he looked like he was going to cry.

Daddy said, "I should have paid more attention. She never said anything. Is the other eye going to be all right? No wonder she thought she was going blind."

"Yes," said Dr. Harvey. "I believe the right eye is going to heal quite nicely. It's too bad she did not tell you sooner. With proper treatment, the eye probably could have been saved if we had known about it in time. But there's no point in blaming yourself. Ella Mae did not want to worry you."

"She was worried about the money. We have been pretty strapped with Granny and Garvin being sick so long. But I aim to take care of this without her having to worry about it. I am going to sell the farm at Grassy Creek. It won't bring much, but it will get us out of debt."

Mary Lou came over to stand beside her father. She could see that he was very upset. "What's the matter, Daddy? Isn't Mommy going to get well?"

Avery put his arm around his little girl. "Of course she's going to get well. She just won't be able to see as well as she did before. But she will get along just fine as soon as she gets home and sees how well you younguns have gotten along with Mrs. Howell."

Mary Lou did not understand all that the men had been talking about, but she could tell that daddy did not want to talk about it anymore. She would wait and talk to Ben. He was older. Maybe he would explain what had happened to their Mother. In the meantime, she figured that she had better pray.

It was two weeks before Mae was able to come home, and even then she was too weak to take over all the housework. But she and Avery both wanted their house to themselves again, and Ben and Mary Lou were ready for their mother's cooking. Jo scarcely would leave Mae's side long enough for her to change her clothes.

When Eileen offered to take a week's vacation from her job, Mae did not argue. She told Eileen that she was determined to assume light housekeeping as soon as possible.

One day, Ben came home from school very upset. He stormed into the house, changed his clothes, and went to the barn without saying a word to anyone.

"Well, what got into him?" Eileen wondered aloud.

Mae looked at Eileen. "I don't know, but maybe he will be over it by the time he comes in to supper. You know, teenagers sometimes let their emotions run out of control, and often the less that is said, the better."

Avery soon noticed Ben's mood and called him aside to see how he should handle the anger he saw in his son's face. He had been concerned about Ben's grades lately and already had spoken to him about it.

"What's the matter, Son? Did you have a bad time today?"

"Aw, Dad," Ben began, fighting to hold back the tears. "Mr. Fulton's not fair!"

"Why do you say that?"

Ben struggled to keep his voice level. "Well, we were supposed to have a notebook to work in for Mr. Fulton's class, and I didn't have one. I forgot to tell you that I needed it by today." He crossed his arms over his chest as he continued. "Freddie Issacs had an extra one that he offered to sell me. I gave him seventy-five cents for it. They only cost forty-nine cents at Woolworth's, but I needed it today."

"That shouldn't have made you mad. It will teach you to think ahead the next time."

"But, Dad," Ben continued, "when Mr. Fulton called on Freddie for his report, Freddie said he couldn't give it because I had stolen his notebook. Mr. Fulton asked me about it, and I said I bought it. Freddie lied and said I didn't and where would I get seventy-five cents because I was just a farm boy." Ben's tears slid down his cheeks.

Avery knew Mrs. Issacs. She was president of the PTA and never hesitated to let people know that she was somebody. "Yes, Son, you are a farm boy, but that's nothing to be ashamed of. I believe over half of the boys in your class are 'just farm boys.' Pay no attention to Freddie. I bet Mr. Fulton knows what kind of a boy he is."

"Freddie said he could prove the book was his and told Mr. Fulton to look in the back of the book. Mr. Fulton made me bring the book to him, and when he looked in the back, there was Freddie's name. And he believed him, Daddy." Ben cried harder.

Avery put his arm across the boy's shoulder. He knew he had to be careful about his next words.

"And that's not all," Ben sobbed. "Mr. Fulton gave me a lecture in front of the whole class and then gave me an 'E' for the whole project. You believe me, don't you, Dad?"

"Yes, I believe you."

"I'm going to get even with Freddie. Just because his mother is a big shot with all the teachers, he thinks he can do anything and get away with it."

Avery didn't say any more, but that night after supper, he got out his Bible and turned to Romans chapter twelve. He read, "'Do not repay anyone evil for evil. Be careful to do what is right in the eyes of everybody. If it is possible, as far as it depends on you, live at peace with everyone. Do not take revenge... "It is mine to avenge; I will repay," says the Lord.' So you see, Ben. You don't need to do anything to Freddie. I know you didn't steal the book. God knows you didn't steal the book. God also knows Freddie lied. Now, let God take care of it."

After the Bible reading, Eileen laughed as she and her mother started to tidy up the kitchen. "Dad, do you want me to write a letter to Mr. Fulton the way I did when Ben was demoted to third grade the first year we came to Maryland?"

"No. I think I can take care of this myself. I have to go out that way tomorrow evening anyhow. In fact, I have to pass right by Mr. Fulton's house. Sure will be glad when Ben graduates. I'm tired of going to school at my age!"

Ella Mae soon regained her strength enough for Eileen to return to her job. The summer was coming to a close, the garden was about finished, and canning was done. It was time for the fall revival. Mae insisted that Avery put their name down to host one of the cottage prayer meetings that would prepare their hearts for the time of spiritual refreshing the revivals usually brought. This year, the congregation had decided to ask their new pastor to do the preaching instead of inviting a visiting preacher to come. This would give them a chance to get better acquainted with him and be more like family as they worshipped together.

An unusually large group of members arrived at the Brown house on the evening they were scheduled for prayer services. Ella Mae was delighted to see so many of her friends. She had sorely missed them in the time she had been unable to attend church.

After a few minutes of catching up on neighborhood news, the group quickly came to the business of prayer, for which they had gathered. Ella Mae had come to the meeting with the needs of her children heavy on her heart. With the older children away from the influence of home and the many temptations they were facing in their various places of work and living, she felt a mighty need for praying a hedge of protection around them. And then there was Ben. Ella Mae prayed for him often. He seemed so alone since his brothers were gone, and there was not much chance for making friends of the sort he needed. Most of the farm boys his age were busy with girls, and so far, this did not seem to be of interest to him. Ella Mae thought this was something to be thankful for.

As different members of the group spoke about the burdens on their hearts and called out the names of people they needed to pray for, Ella Mae listened. She was not one to speak out in front of others, but tonight she had a definite urge to ask for prayer for her children. Tears gushed from her eyes as she tried to articulate what was on her heart, but she was not embarrassed. These were folks who understood what it was to have children out in the world and some not always living as close to the Lord as they should.

Avery mentioned to Mae the next day that he was not very enthused about this revival. He liked their new preacher as a person, but his preaching was a little different from the hell-fire and damnation preaching Avery was partial to. Their pastor seldom raised his voice, and Avery hated to admit his bias against young seminary preachers. Mae had to remind him constantly that their son Riley was young. He had decided not to stay in seminary to finish his education, and she strongly regretted it.

At the revival, the singing was as robust as usual. By the time the music was finished, the room was full, as people had filed into the few remaining seats.

The sermon was about the one lost sheep and the ninety and nine that were safe. Nothing they hadn't heard before. And it was presented (so Avery commented) in a sort of matter-of-fact way.

Then it was time for the hymn of invitation, that part of the evening toward which all of their efforts and prayers had been directed. This was when everyone hoped that the ones who needed to let Jesus into their hearts would come forward and acknowledge the decisions they had made. Someone might want to become a member of the church, some might feel the need to renew their allegiance to the Lord, and others might want to come forward to pray.

The pastor asked everyone to bow their heads and be in prayer as he urged those who needed to make decisions to do so. Ella Mae was sitting near the front beside Avery. She sensed someone walking past her toward the front of the church, but she did not raise her eyes until Avery pressed her hand. When she looked up and saw Ben kneeling with the pastor, she thought for a moment she would faint. Such joy filled her heart that she could not contain it. "Praise God!" she shouted. Clapping her hands and calling forth praises, she cried aloud, "This is what I've been praying for. Thank You, Lord Jesus! Amen and Amen!"

It seemed to Mae that she floated up the aisle to kneel beside her boy. Avery was right behind her, and soon everyone was rejoicing with them. Church members had watched Ben as he came to Sunday school and church, but they had not realized that he never had professed his faith in Jesus as God's Son and his Savior.

Ben's conversion sowed the seeds for others to examine their relationship with the Lord, and there were one or two others who decided to trust Christ to forgive their sins and several rededications among the young people of the church that night.

After the service, Mae's friends were liberal with their hugs, and tears stood in many eyes as they thought of their own children. It was a night of sweet fellowship.

The next Sunday, they had a baptism after the morning service. And that night, Mae held Avery's hand as he thanked the Lord for sending them their young pastor and for using him to speak quietly to Ben's heart. He added a plea for forgiveness for his attitude.

"Mae, I think it's about time we had the pastor and his young wife over for dinner. I'll ask him next Sunday."

"You needn't bother," Mae replied with a smile. "I already did."

CHAPTER 16

Letters and Visits

MAE LOOKED AT the letter from her sister-in-law. Harriet had written to say Faye had moved from their home into an apartment with another girl. Faye had not liked the fact that Uncle Bill had set a curfew for her to be in at night. She was working hard but also playing hard. There were other things as well. Harriet did not elaborate on these "other things." These worried Mae more than the ones she did include.

Mae had hesitated to share this news with Avery, believing he would say to her, "I told you so!" But because she never had kept things from him, she'd reluctantly handed him the letter.

Whether it was the fact that he was busy trying to adjust to changes in his job or that he realized Mae had enough on her mind with Ben getting ready for his senior year, all he'd said was, "Looks like we'll have to pray a little harder."

Mae sat on the swing, waiting for Ben to return from the mailbox. She was not expecting anything special, but she needed a break from working in the kitchen all morning. The garden seemed to be outdoing itself this year, and the abundance of vegetables to be canned seemed never to stop. Last week it was green beans, and today it was tomatoes. She was grateful for the generous provision of food for the coming winter and more than grateful for this moment of rest.

Ben arrived and bounded up on the porch to hand her a circular and a few pieces of mail for Avery. A pretty postcard with a picture of rolling hills that reminded her of North Carolina brought a smile to her face. She turned it over to see the card was addressed to Mr. and Mrs. Brown and was from Riley. It was about time he got in touch. They had not heard a word since he left for the south at the beginning of summer.

As Ben went inside, Mae read the card: "Dear Mom and Dad, Just a note to tell you that I got married this morning. Her name is Anna Wilson. I think you might know some of her people. I know this sounds sudden. She is a lovely girl, and I know you will love her. We will be home to see you when I can get time off from my new job. Love, Riley."

Mae was still sitting in stunned silence when Avery came in for dinner. He expected her to be putting dinner on the table and looked to see if she was ill. She handed him the postcard without a word and waited to hear his response. Surprisingly, there was none.

Questions repeated themselves over and over in Mae's head, with no one to answer them. What had Riley done? What about his schooling? Who was this girl? Did they know her family? He had only been gone from home a few months. How could he have met and married someone so quickly? Who would marry young people without finding out about them? Was he bringing her home? Where would they live? What new job was he talking about? What was Avery thinking? Why didn't he say something? Was he angry?

When Avery still said nothing, Mae went in to put dinner on the table. She moved automatically, like a zombie. It was a good thing everything was ready and all she had to do was place the food on the table. Mae put Jo in her seat, and Ben and Mary Lou slid into their places, chattering away about their big brother. Ben had looked at the postcard as he walked from the mailbox, so he knew about the wedding. He and Mary Lou already had discussed it. They kept watching Mother and Daddy, obviously waiting to see what they had to say.

The children quieted down while Avery asked the blessing. Then as the food was passed around the table, questions began. There were plenty of questions but no answers.

Mae could think of nothing but her son. She thought back to the day he was born. He made her number of children even; there were two boys and two girls. Eileen was a jealous two year old, who demanded equal attention with the new baby. Faye loved playing the little mother and remained at her elbow to make sure she was changing his diaper on time and keeping him warm enough. The tiny cabin where they lived on New River was beginning to be crowded. Jenny, her dear friend and sister-in-law, had taken the children to her house for a few days to give Mae time to rest. Of course, Avery had strutted around like he had done it all! Well, he wasn't strutting today. What was he thinking?

Mae had worried about Riley as he grew and as more children were added to their family. He was a happy child, contented with whatever the other children wanted him to play. He learned at an early age to stay away from Foster, who seemed to get a perverse pleasure from tormenting him. Foster would pretend to hurt one of the girls or one of the animals, and Riley would fly into him with both fists. The only time he showed anger was when there was an injustice or injury of some kind. Whenever there was an unpleasant task to be performed, Riley would end up doing it, without complaint. Although Avery tried to divide the work on their little farm according to the children's ages and sizes, somehow Riley ended up with the dirtiest, most unpleasant chores to be done. Yet, as docile as Riley seemed, the others soon learned they could only push him so far.

What had caused him to run off and get married? Mae thought about his leaving home. Perhaps "run off" was not the correct word. He had not left without their permission. He simply had stated that he did not like living in Maryland and wanted to see what there was ahead for him "back home."

Avery and Ella Mae always had held to the rule that once the children were out of high school, they were on their own and would need to earn their own living. This was especially true of the boys. The girls could stay at home until they were married, but the boys needed to find their place in life and no longer depend on their parents for support.

Mae thought back to the day Riley had appeared at their door, suitcase in hand. He was supposed to be in college, and it was just the middle of his second year. Avery had seen him walking down the lane and come to the house to see what was the matter. Riley explained that he had quit school, not to return there again. He was attending Bible class when the professor announced to the class that he did not believe in the virgin birth of our Lord and that it was not necessary for them to believe in it either. That was enough for Riley and several other students to leave. Riley said that he did not mind waiting on tables for his meals or missing out on sports in order to study or doing his own laundry, but he was not going to listen to someone blaspheme his Lord. How could Jesus be the Son of God if He was just the son of an ordinary man? He would be no different from anyone else. And so, Riley came home. If Jesus was not God's Son, what was there to preach about?

Avery and Mae did not argue with Riley, although Mae was disappointed. What would Riley do if he did not finish his education? The days were passing swiftly when a God-called man would be asked to fill a pulpit without an education beyond high school. Avery, however, never had been sure that Riley really was called to preach. Maybe this was God's way of telling him just to get a job and go to work.

Mae thought back to the times before they left Grassy Creek, when she had listened as Riley talked with Granny about his desire to become a preacher. Granny was ever his ardent supporter, advising him about ways he must look after the needs of his congregation. She never doubted that he would have a church someday and began instilling ideas into his head regarding his pastoral duties. She was especially adamant about visiting the sick and elderly.

After one such time of instruction, Mae went to gather eggs and saw Riley take his place on an old stump out in the pasture. The cows had heard his voice and approached the pasture fence, chewing their cuds and swishing their tails to keep the flies away from their backs. The old collie dog was lying down by the stump while the chickens slowly walked over, pecking insects from the grass as they came.

Riley announced his favorite hymn and motioned for the old dog to stand. He lazily stood to his feet, strolled around to the other side of the stump, and dropped to the ground again. Riley threw his head back and sang to the top of his voice. As he directed his "choir," the chickens responded here and there with a slight flutter of their wings and continued scratching and pecking at anything that moved near their feet.

Mae paused inside the door of the chicken house, her basket of eggs across her arm. Riley chose to preach about Nicodemus, the tax collector, who came to see Jesus by night. When he came to the place where Jesus said, "Ye must be born again!" Riley thundered it out so strongly that one of the cows backed away from the fence and with a low "moo," walked to the stream, lowered her head, and began to drink.

Riley pointed at the cow. "All right, Mrs. Cow. Go ahead and walk away. If you turn your back on Jesus, you will need that water, because you will burn in hell without Him! Just remember, He said, "You *must* be born again!" Riley then said a closing prayer and left to do his chores.

Ella Mae thought about that time and many others when she heard the children tease him about his "preaching." He had not preached to the chickens since they moved to Maryland, and not a lot had been said about his decision to go to college at Wake Forest. He had filled out all the applications himself and worked with Uncle Carl to get a little financial aid, but it was up to him to come up with money for his books and other expenses.

Questions kept running through Ella Mae's mind—questions without answers. Where was he living? How could he support a wife? By bedtime, she had another headache, and still Avery had said nothing. Mae did the only thing she knew to do: lay her burdens at the feet of the Master. Riley was His child, and surely He would take care of His own.

The next morning, Avery came to her before going to the barn, slipped his arm around her waist, and half jokingly asked, "Have you prayed about this, Mae?"

She looked down. How many times had she asked that same question of her husband? "That's all we can do, isn't it?" She looked up and gave him a quick kiss before he turned and went out the door. He obviously was as concerned as she but knew there really was nothing more they could do. When children left their mother's domain, it was called "cutting the apron strings." What was it called when they stepped away from their father's care? Just as long as he never stepped away from the care of the heavenly Father, and she knew Riley never would, things would work out.

Ella Mae relearned a lesson that she had known for a long time: no matter how old your children are or what they do, one never ceases to be a parent. The children might grow too old to listen or heed their parents' advice, and there would come a time when they had to take up their own way of life without interference from their parents, but they always would need prayers said on their behalf.

Riley had made a decision, albeit an impulsive one, and he would have to live with it. They would welcome this newcomer to the family, and Mae was sure they would learn to love her. If Riley did, how could they not?

Two days later, a letter arrived from Faye, announcing that she was going to marry a doctor. She said he was everything she always had wanted, and life was going to be wonderful. He already had been accepted at the hospital and only had two more years of residency before he would be on the staff as a full doctor. Faye acknowledged that she knew they might be disappointed because he was a Catholic. Then the rest of the letter was filled with reasons why this did not matter and how happy she was going to be. In closing, she asked if they thought they might come to the wedding. It would be in two weeks, just as soon as she graduated from nursing school. Faye also suggested that they could stay with Uncle Bill and Aunt Harriet, "although they are very mad with me right now, for some ridiculous reason. But I'm sure they would be glad to have you visit."

Mae laid the letter aside, shaking her head at the thought of how Avery would react to this one. Well, Faye was going to see her dreams come true. Was that such a good thing? Mae wondered where the Lord was in all of these plans. She desperately wanted to ask her daughter if she had prayed about this. Somehow she felt she already knew the answer.

Avery also shook his head when he finished with the letter. "You know what I'm going to say, don't you? If you really want to go, I'll manage to get the money together. I would like to see Bill and Harriet, but I don't think I would fit in Faye's world."

Mae could not believe she would fit in either. She sat down to write to her daughter but could not seem to find the words she wanted to say. She ended up writing to Harriet instead. While she was at it, she penned a short note to Foster and his wife, informing them of the upcoming wedding. By the time she was finished with that chore, and writing was a chore, it was time to feed the chickens and gather the eggs.

Time went by, and the letter to Faye had not been written. It seemed like such a long time since she had gone away from their little farm. Eileen had been the one who had kept in touch with her sister. Mae wondered if Eileen knew that Faye was getting married to the doctor of her dreams. Maybe Mae would wait until she heard from Eileen and then she would write.

The very next week, another letter arrived from Detroit. Mae turned the envelope over a couple of times before she opened it. There was a strange return address in the corner: Mr. and Mrs. Alvan Cooper. Who could that be? Perhaps this was someone who was giving Faye a wedding shower.

Mae opened the letter and read:

Dear Mom and Dad,

You will be surprised to know that I am now Mrs. Alvan Cooper. I was going to marry my doctor friend, but at the wedding shower, I met and fell in love with the most wonderful man anyone could imagine. Since he declared it was love at first sight with him also, what could I do? It would not have been fair to marry one man while being in love with someone else, would it?

Al owns a car dealership for General Motors and sells Oldsmobiles. The only problem is that we will be living in California, and that seems like a long way from home. The good news is that we are coming home before we go out there. I want you to meet him, and I know that you will love him as much as I do.

Our plans are to leave here at the end of next week. I have to finish up all the loose ends here at school, and of course, I have to make peace with Aunt Harriet and Uncle Bill. We should be at your house by Thursday at the latest. I can't wait to see

you both and all the little ones. Do you think Eileen
could come home for a few days while we are there?
Will you ask her? Must close and see you soon.
Love,
Mrs. Alvan Cooper

Mae scarcely could believe what she was reading
and picked up the letter to go over it once more to
make sure of what it said. Not one word about what
happened to her doctor friend or all the plans for her
wedding. Not one word to ask if it was agreeable for
them to come at this time. Naturally, Mae reasoned, her
children knew they were welcome at their home at any
hour of the day or night, but it would have been nice
to be acknowledged.

Mae tried not to let any annoyance show as she broke
the news to Avery. But the truth was that their family
was changing too fast to suit her. There had not been
time to adjust her heart and mind to the fact that Riley
was married and would be bringing a new person into
their life to get to know and, hopefully, love. At least she
was from the south. Why did Faye have to make such a
drastic move and bring a stranger into the family?

Of course, Mae realized she was being silly. At least
Faye had finished her nurses training. She was qualified
to take care of herself, but now, it seemed, she would
not have to. One thing she could be thankful for was
that Faye was coming home before moving to California.

My, that seemed a long distance away. How long would it be before they would see her again?

Mae looked at Avery. "Thank goodness Eileen seems to be settled down for awhile. I don't know how I would handle it if she got some flighty notion of getting married!"

Avery just said, "Humph!"

It did not take long for Thursday to roll around. There had been phone calls to Eileen, who also had heard the news, and house cleaning to be done. Mae did more than was necessary. Mary Lou gladly gave up her bedroom and helped straighten everything out to make a comfortable and pleasing room for the new bride and groom.

Mae could see the shiny red convertible come around the barn. She quickly took off her apron and smoothed her hair before hurrying out to welcome Faye and her new husband to their home and family.

Faye hugged her mother as if she never would let go. Mae was not in a hurry to break away either, saying, "Has it really been five years since we have seen you? I can tell you now, I don't want it to be that long again!"

When the two had feasted their eyes on one another long enough, they turned to look at the tall, good-looking, young man standing beside the car.

Faye proceeded to introduce her new husband to her mother. She obviously was proud of her husband but wanted to make sure he appreciated what a special mother she had. It was clear to Ella Mae that Faye was confident of her conquest, and judging by the outward appearances, she had done well for herself. Mae prayed in her heart that he was as fine as his clothes and his car. She determined to treat him like one of the family.

Avery arrived to add his congratulations to the young groom. He said that he felt that any man should be grateful for such a companion as Faye. It seemed to Mae that he hugged Faye a little tighter than she was used to, but no one else noticed.

Mae noticed how grown up Faye looked and wondered if Faye noticed a difference in them. She knew the years were beginning to show on Avery and her.

Avery returned to work, and Al and Faye unpacked the car and settled their things where Ella Mae directed them, talking all the while about their wedding and the trip from Michigan. Their plans were to stay until the following Wednesday and then head to California, where Al's business was needing his attention.

Eileen and Garvin arrived about the same time as Ben and Mary Lou came in from school. There seemed to be a lot of commotion for a few minutes, until all the introductions were made and hugs were distributed all around. Mae knew Faye and Eileen were eager to be off to themselves for a few minutes and urged them to sit on the front porch while she began to put the finishing touches on supper.

Garvin went to the barn to help his dad finish the milking. "Just to show him that I've not lost my touch," he joked.

Al followed Ben to the barn and watched as he began his chores. As soon as the milking was finished and the cows let out to pasture, the men gathered around the new Oldsmobile in the yard. Al delighted in showing off all the new features and demonstrating how the top folded back and then could be raised again to change the car from a convertible to a sedan. Avery could see that he had the gift of gab that a salesman needed and had little doubt that he would be able to make a good living. Perhaps Faye had made a wise choice after all.

Conversation around the table never slowed down once the food was passed. Avery wondered how they could talk so much and still eat, but the platters of fried chicken and bowls of green beans and mashed potatoes seemed to need refilling almost immediately. Bowls of chicken gravy followed by plates of hot biscuits and platters of fresh tomatoes and baked apples circled the table several times.

Their new son-in-law might turn up his nose at the lack of indoor plumbing, but it was plain to be seen that he was well pleased by Ella Mae's cooking. Whether it was the abundance of good food added to good conversation or the excitement of seeing each other again, the family was tired that first night and did not stay up late.

The next morning, Al decided that he and Garvin should take the children on a trip in the convertible on Saturday. Gettysburg was not that far away, and since he was a Civil War buff, he was excited to see the battlefield for himself. He thought Garvin would be good company and said it would not hurt any of them to learn a little more history.

Mae could see from the planning that he wanted to get away from the house for awhile. But she also credited him for realizing that she and Eileen would like to have some time with Faye by themselves.

A tired and hungry bunch rolled out of the car Saturday evening. They did not even have to be told to wash up and head for the table. Mae was happy to hear that Ben and Mary Lou were thrilled with riding in the beautiful car. It had proved to be a very hot day, and they said that the wind blowing in their faces was a great sensation. Apparently it was only when they stopped for a red light or some other reason that the hot sun reflecting from the red leather caused them to squirm and wish for some shade.

Faye and her husband declined to go with the family to Sunday school and church the next morning. Their reasoning was that Eileen had to return to her job and would be leaving that evening. Of course, this gave Eileen a reason to stay home also.

Al had brought along his set of golf clubs, and the game greatly interested Garvin. So he stayed home, too. They went over into the pasture field, where the ground was fairly level, and Al taught him the rudiments of the game.

"Cow-Pasture Pool," Avery called it.

Mae did not argue, but she was greatly disappointed that the children chose other things instead of worship. She really wanted them exposed to the preaching of the Word. But she also had to admit that she wanted to show off her fine, grown children to her friends. She well knew the Bible said, "Thou shalt not envy," but she had a hard time with her heart that morning as she looked around the congregation and saw several of her friends in attendance with their grown children. Only her special friend, Mrs. Wells, seemed to understand how she felt.

Time for their departure arrived too quickly for Mae. California was indeed a long distance away. It probably would be quite some time before they would see their daughter again. Still, once the final good-byes were said and the red car disappeared around the barn, it seemed good to have things back to normal.

Time passed and it was a year later that Riley and Anna arrived with their new baby around the end of August. Riley had been invited to conduct a two week revival at a nearby church. Avery said it was in view of a call for him to be their minister. Even with the extra work, it was an enjoyable time for the family. Mae was glad most of the gardening work was finished, and the heavy work of canning was almost over. She managed to get most of her work done by dinnertime, and the afternoon was free for visiting.

Jo enjoyed playing with the baby, and their visit was a welcome break in the long summer days. There were few children to play with on the farm, and Mary Lou always had her head stuck in a book, so a new baby that she could play with was a glad change for her too. The baby still took long naps and Anna made sure she was not disturbed so she would not be restless during the revival services at night.

The more Mae saw of her daughter-in-law, the better she liked her. She could tell that Anna was a hard worker and took great pride in the appearance of Riley and the baby. She could tell from his attitude and looks that her son was happy, and according to him, he had married the best cook in all of Virginia.

Supper was ready each evening as soon as Avery finished his work for the day. One of the deacons from the church where the revival was being held stopped by and picked up Riley to go visit some of the church members and some prospects for the church. Later, Avery took the women and children to the service. He and Ella Mae tried not to look too proud as Riley mounted the steps to the pulpit, but it was evident that they were happy with their son.

After the first week, Mae did not have to worry about the evening meal, as one of the church members had Riley and his family for supper each night before the service. Mae thanked God for the call to preach that had been extended to Riley. Surely God was with him, and it was evident by the power with which he preached. Her prayer life was busy as she bathed him in prayer and remembered to pray for all of her children to know the Lord and His salvation.

The revival ended with a baptismal service on Sunday afternoon and the usual dinner on the grounds. Boards stretched across sawhorses on the church grounds groaned with the many dishes of fresh vegetables and fried chicken and ham and the many desserts that the women of the church had prepared. Mae was glad to see several of their friends from the church she and Avery attended at the service. All together, it was a lovely day to enjoy and remember.

The visit ended early the next morning as Riley and his little family left for the hills of Virginia. The good time of worshipping the Lord and visiting with family was a welcome change, but now it was time to return to normal living. One last wave and the duties of everyday life called for their time and efforts. Time would tell whether the church would call Riley to be their pastor. Meanwhile there was work waiting for them at home.

CHAPTER 17

A New Dream

AVERY COULD TELL that he was going to have to find other employment soon. Both Garvin and Riley were gone, and Ben soon would graduate from high school. Since Avery would not have the extra help with the farm work, Mr. Randolph would be requiring the house they were in for someone with sons to help on the farm. He had not said anything to Avery about moving, but that's just the way farms were operated. Men who had sons old enough to help were the ones owners were seeking, and goodness knows there were enough men looking for good places to work.

The agriculture teacher at the high school had become one of Avery's friends and advised him of a farm one of the teachers owned that needed a manager. This teacher and her brother had inherited the family farm, and since neither of them had the faintest idea about farming, things were going from bad to worse. This seemed like the answer to Avery's dilemma. He would not have to go searching for work, and Mr. Randolph would not have to ask him to leave.

An agreement soon was reached, and once again, Ella Mae was packing boxes and adjusting to a new home. The two-story house was not too bad, but again, there was no indoor plumbing. The good point about this location was that Ben and Mary Lou did not have to change schools, and they would not need to change churches. This time, Ella Mae's life only changed in regards to the events of the family.

The year passed swiftly, and it soon was time to renew their contract. Avery could see that it had not been a profitable year. In fact, he thought he probably had lost money. The hay crop had been poor from the year before, and he'd had to buy hay to feed the stock through the winter. Then several pieces of harness for the horses had to be replaced, adding to expenses he had not expected when he took over the farm. It was time for another change.

Ella Mae never had been really happy about living on this farm. She hated seeing Avery come in from work every day looking so defeated. He was a good farmer, and somewhere there was a place for them to earn a good salary. This had been a good farm at one time, but several years of neglect and mismanagement had taken their toll, and it was simply worn out. Even the garden did not produce very well.

The past year had seen several changes in their family. Jo had been old enough to begin school. Mary Lou had taught her to print the ABCs over the summer and was sounding out words with her so that she had a good start in first grade. Eileen had married a man who was much older than she, but both Mae and Avery liked him very much, and unlike their other married children, Eileen and her husband lived close enough for frequent visits. Ben had graduated from high school and, anxious to earn some money of his own, had secured a job in the same town where Garvin and Eileen lived. In fact, he roomed with Garvin. That left only Mary Lou and Jo at home with Mae and Avery.

Mae was more than ready when Avery approached her near the end of February with his little account book and wanted to talk. However, she was surprised when he told her he had found a little farm that he wanted to buy and asked if she would like to go with him to look it over.

Where had he found the money to buy a farm? Mae wondered. She looked at him with eyes full of questions.

"Yes, I have prayed about it," Avery said before she even could get the question fixed in her mind.

They laughed together as Mae got her coat and wiped tears of excitement from her eyes.

"I knew you would ask, so I thought I'd save you the trouble."

As they drove out into the countryside, Avery explained his plans to Mae. He seemed a little pleased with himself, obviously expecting that Mae would like what he had in mind.

"This place is not big enough for us to make a living off of it, but I have been offered a job as a carpenter's helper, and with my salary and what we can make off of a few chickens, we should do all right."

It was a beautiful day, almost like spring, the kind that got one's hopes up that perhaps warm weather was just around the corner. Even if Avery was only daydreaming about buying a farm, it was good to break the routine of daily life.

Mae admired the neat farms they passed as they rode along. A two-story house sitting up on a small incline, surrounded by large maple trees, caught her eye. She could imagine what the place would look like in the summer when those trees were in full leaf. Someday she hoped to live in a house like that.

She was delighted when Avery pulled into the driveway and stopped the car. It gave her a chance to see the house up close. The wraparound porch would be an ideal place for a swing and a rocking chair or two.

Mae made no move to get out of the car. She assumed he was going in to ask the owner for the key to the place where they were going. She was a little startled when Avery came around and opened her door.

"Don't you want to come in and see the house?"

"You mean this is the place you are talking about buying?"

"Well, yes," Avery held the key up for her to see. "But it depends on how you like it, of course."

"Oh, Avery!" She couldn't say another word and couldn't get out of the car fast enough. She stood on the wide cement porch, almost afraid to breath. Avery unlocked the door and stood aside as his wife stepped into a sunny kitchen, spacious enough to eat in, complete with a practically new cook stove and a sink under wide windows that overlooked a large backyard. A pantry opened off to one side with an opposite door leading to the steps that went down to a basement.

An archway led into another room that contained a space heater large enough to comfortably heat the entire house. A small foyer led to the front porch and to an adjoining room open on one side to a stairway leading to the second floor. Mae guessed this was "the company room."

Mae slowly climbed the stairs to a hallway that opened to four bedrooms. She opened each door gingerly and visualized Mary Lou and Jo having their own rooms. And, of course, there was a nice, big room for Avery and her. But when she opened the last door, she almost collapsed. There were not four bedrooms but three—and a bathroom! Indoor plumbing! Could it be true?

Visions of the first house Avery had taken her to when they moved from North Carolina to Maryland came unbidden to her mind. Could this truly be the home she had dreamed of, instead of the old log house they had lived in for two years? She turned to Avery, unable to say a word.

"I thought you'd like it. And you are getting too old to have to run outdoors in all kinds of weather each time you need to use the bathroom."

She hardly could tear herself away from the upstairs, as she already was placing their furniture about and deciding what kinds of curtains each room must have; but Avery wanted to show her the rest of the farm. They descended the stairs and went out the front door.

Mae was delighted with the view from the front porch. The land across the highway sloped down to another farmhouse, where she could see smoke lazily curling from the chimney. Neighbors within walking distance! She was not one to gad about, but it was nice to know there would be someone near in case of need.

She walked to the end of the porch and looked out over the land that led past a meadow to some woods. Then she followed Avery across the porch and around the side of the house to the back porch. Mae could envision the flower bed that she would plant on that side of the house—dahlias, zinnias, marigolds, petunias, and whatever other flowers would make a showing to any passersby. A path led to a gate in the fence that opened to the meadow. There was a space near the fence for a garden. Mae almost could see rows of vegetables growing there.

Someone had left a clothesline strung between two posts in the backyard. A small shed that perhaps housed a lawn mower or garden tools stood near the driveway that wound around to the barn.

"Mae, I am going to build you a nice chicken house where that little shed stands, and it will reach all the way to the barn. That way, when the weather is bad and I need to go milk our cow, I can walk through the chicken house and take care of them at the same time."

Mae remembered the chicken house Avery had built for her in Grassy Creek. She would have a few suggestions to make before he started this one. She caught herself thinking ahead as if they really were buying the farm. She did not know how they could manage it financially, but wouldn't it be wonderful if by some miracle they could? Avery had said, "Leave it to me." And she would do just that. But a little niggle of anxiety lingered in her mind.

They continued their tour of the farm, with Avery pointing out the boundary lines of what they would own. The barn that would house their cow seemed in good repair, and on the back side was a pen suitable for hogs. Mae was glad it was far enough away so that the odor would not penetrate the house.

Avery came over and put his arm around her waist. "God certainly moves in mysterious ways, His wonders to perform. This seems to be the answer to our prayers for a suitable place that would meet our needs and, at the same time, answer the prayers of the owners for a buyer."

"How do you know they prayed about selling this farm?"

"Do you remember the request for the sick mother of one of our church members not long ago?"

"Yes, but she died." Mae had not known the woman who was so ill, but Avery knew her son, who happened to be in his Sunday school class.

"Well, her son inherited the property, and he cannot afford to keep it. He approached me about it a few weeks ago, saying I could buy it at a good price because he did not have to go through a realtor and it would be a quick sale. What do you think? Will it do?"

"It will do most wonderfully!" Mae threw her arms around Avery's neck. "Could we move tomorrow?"

Mae was not serious, but she wanted to let him see that she really did not like where they were living and did like the home he had chosen for them. It was like the sweet savor spoken about in the Bible. Avery would not have to wonder about his decision this time.

Their ride home was a journey of planning and dreaming.

Chapter 18

One More Time

THE TIME FOR moving to their new home appeared to drag on forever. On the other hand, it seemed to fly by. When Avery informed his employers that he could not work for them any longer, they seemed to be greatly relieved. It happened that they wanted to sell the farm, as they realized it was too much for them to operate, but they hated to tell Mr. Brown they could not renew his contract for another year.

And so Ella Mae drug out her packing boxes for what she hoped would be the final time. She could not believe how smoothly everything was working out. Surely God was in this move and they could put down roots now, like their friends had done years before.

Their friends at church were happy for them, even though it meant they would be leaving their present

189

place of worship. They would be going back to the church they had first attended when they moved from North Carolina. In a sense, it was like a homecoming, with many friends waiting to welcome them back into their fellowship.

Mary Lou and Jo had to change schools, but they were young, and it would not take them long to adjust. They were as excited about their new home as their mother and father were. Mary Lou scarcely could believe that she would have a whole room to herself. Mae even allowed her to choose the wallpaper she wanted, a lovely white background sprinkled with large, red roses that seemed to transform the room into a garden. Of course, Jo wanted paper just like Mary Lou's, until Mae showed her a design with kittens frolicking all over it.

The smell of homemade wallpaper paste filled the house for several days, and Mae measured and fitted each piece in place. She was able to find enough white curtains for the windows from ones they had used previously. Her sewing machine and ironing board were kept ready to use for any that needed to be adjusted to the proper length and then pressed.

Getting settled in was a busy but happy time. They met over the supper table to relate all that happened each day. Their bodies were tired, but they had happy hearts and faces.

Mary Lou was pleased to be welcomed to the new school by some of her classmates who went to the same church they were now attending. The bus driver was a man who had worked on the farm near their former home, and knew Daddy very well. He remembered when Jo was just a baby, and now that she was a grown-up second grader, he made sure she got to the proper room. He took pleasure in introducing her to her new teacher.

Since the weather had turned warm, the open windows carried the scent of the lilac bushes into the freshly-scrubbed rooms. When they went to bed each night, the smells of spring and odor of clean rooms seemed to mingle and speak of the peace and harmony of God's watch care and love over their family. Mae sighed with pure joy and thanksgiving as she snuggled against Avery's strong back. He did not fail to acknowledge her presence.

The next few months were busy ones. Avery went to his work as a carpenter's helper each day and hurried home to put in a little time on various things that needed to be done before dark. There was the barn to be cleaned and a stall prepared for their cow, who soon would be delivering a calf for them to raise or sell. The garden area had to be cleared and the ground prepared for plowing and planting. The familiar odor of spread manure filled the air.

In the evenings, after supper was over and the children were settled for the night, Avery and Ella Mae made plans for the new chicken house that needed to be built as soon as possible. Mae had brought a few hens from the last farm and kept them in the little shed in the backyard. These hens supplied them with enough eggs to eat and a few for cooking. But they needed room for many more. They needed to be ready to be real chicken farmers if they were going to have added income to supplement Avery's wages.

Garvin and Ben came home almost every weekend to help with odd jobs Avery had ready for them. Once the chicken house was started, they made sure to come prepared to put in a solid day's work every Saturday until it was finished and filled with young pullets, almost ready to begin laying eggs.

Their new home proved to be everything Mae had dreamed of. She never had been more content. It was true they had to watch their money, but hadn't they always? There was something intangible but wonderful about owning your own property.

The first year seemed to fly by, and summer saw a bountiful garden that produced a cellar full of canned goods. Mae was pleased that everyone was staying well and healthy.

Avery still had his habit of asking people to come home with him for dinner or supper after church on Sundays. And, as always, most of the time his invitation was accepted. Mae had learned to have just a little extra prepared on Sunday so that it was only a matter of a short while before a wonderful meal was on the table. In the summer, when the garden was full of vegetables, this was an easy task. Later in the year, Mae was thankful for the gleaming rows of canned vegetables and fruit that she could raid for a tasty meal. She was glad for the fellowship those Sundays and especially glad for the men who came to talk with Avery.

Avery never complained about his going out to work. In fact, he was most grateful that he had a job to add to what they needed to keep this farm. But once in a while, she noticed how he lovingly ran his hands down over the head of their cow. She saw how much he enjoyed plowing and putting in the garden. He would stop and pick up a handful of warm earth and smell it, as a woman might smell a bouquet of flowers. That he was a farmer inside and out was clear to anyone who was observant.

One cold winter day, friends they had known for many years drove out to the farm. They were from the same area of North Carolina where Avery and Ella Mae once had lived. Mae put on a pot of coffee and soon had a tasty supper prepared. She proceeded to carry the food to the living room, where their friends were seated. The men were deep in discussion about the affairs over in Europe, where Hitler seemed to be trying to take over the world.

Avery soon suggested that they turn on the news and see if anything new was happening. They were surprised to hear the voice of President Franklin Delano Roosevelt. It was December 7, 1941, and America had been attacked!

CHAPTER 19

Changes Everywhere

*D*ECEMBER 8 DAWNED just the same as the day before, but that was the only thing that remained as usual. Avery drove to his work place, where men looked at each other with concern and anger on their faces. Ella Mae went about her housework as if in a daze, her mind on her sons, who certainly would be affected by this tremendous event.

The twelve o'clock news broadcast was heard by radio audiences around the country. President Roosevelt spoke of the "day that will live in infamy" and officially declared war on the country of Japan for the bombing of Pearl Harbor. Workers listened with their lunch boxes open, but they forgot to eat. School children were gathered in assemblies to hear words they did not fully comprehend, like, "We have nothing to fear but fear itself." Mothers held their little ones close and breathed the names of their older sons in prayer. They tried to prepare their hearts for what was coming.

Avery and Ella Mae went about their evening chores as usual. The main difference was the silence, as their thoughts were on the news that came in a steady stream from the radio. Ordinarily the radio was not turned on until their work was finished and their day had been discussed around the supper table, but today was different, as details of ships sunk and lives lost changed from hour to hour.

They were still at the table when a car drove up. They opened the door to a gentleman in uniform. He introduced himself as Captain James McCain of the United States Army.

"Mr. Brown, I'll come right to the point. I need your help. As you might guess, I do not have much time to wrap up my personal life, as I will be leaving within the week to report for duty. No doubt but we will now soon be in this war with Germany, as we should have been long ago. But I digress. As I said before, I need your help.

"I have a 600 acre farm with about sixty cows that have to be milked twice a day and three other men who are good workers but know nothing about running a farm. My foreman has left me without notice, and well you can see what a predicament I am in. I have inquired around, and several men have said you would be the best person to take over for me. These are men I can rely on, and if they say you can handle the job, that's good enough for me. Will you come? I will make it well worth your time if you will help me out."

It was obvious that Avery scarcely could believe his ears. He and Captain McCain talked for quite some time as details of his proposal were explained.

The captain must have noticed that Avery kept glancing at his wife because he soon turned his appeal to Ella Mae. "Mrs. Brown, you can understand the need I have for help right away. Ordinarily, I would not pressure your husband for a decision, but I am desperate. I know nothing of farming, having inherited this farm from my mother. I am a city boy, but I have been told your husband is the best farmer in the area and also the most honest man available. You can see how that is important for me. And it will be important for our country as well. Farming will play a big part in the winning of this war, so your husband will be doing his patriotic duty by helping make this farm a most profitable one in ways that only he can do."

Mae was no dummy. She knew this man was trying to influence her husband through her. She recognized the truth of some of what he was saying, but surely there was someone, somewhere, who could do this job as well as Avery. Why must they give up this beloved place just when it was beginning to show signs of being productive?

The Captain tried again. "I will be leaving my wife and two young boys on the farm while I am away. It really would help my peace of mind if I knew there would be people that could be counted on if they ever needed help. The house you would have to live in is probably not as nice as this one. It is an old stone structure that may need some fixing up to suit you. I can assure you that it can be done, even to adding on more space if you find it necessary. I promise you that you will not be sorry if you make this commitment to help me until this hateful war is finished."

"The decision will be Avery's, and he will need to pray before he gives you an answer," Mae finally replied.

Captain McCain had no answer to that stipulation, and after some further talk, he left with Avery's promise to come and look the situation over on the following afternoon.

Long after the children were in bed and asleep, Avery and Ella Mae talked over this sudden interruption of their plans for the future. What should they do? The money was more than he could hope to make for several more years. And it was all free of any expenses. Ella Mae knew it was more than the money that caused Avery's eyes to sparkle. He would be back to farming with decent equipment and a budget to spend on what he saw as necessary, instead of saving and scraping along.

Avery looked at his wife. "It won't hurt to take a look. I'll stop on the way home and see for myself if the picture is as rosy as he says. In the meantime, we had both better do some tall praying. Mae, I know how you feel about this place, and if you don't want me to take this job, we'll just forget it."

"Avery, you know this decision is yours—after you have prayed about it, that is. I do love this place, and I probably will cry if we have to leave it, but I trust you to make the right decision—after you pray about it."

It would be hard to say which one rolled and tossed the most that night, but daylight finally came, and one of the most momentous days of their life slowly began.

Avery took Mae with him to look over everything about the new job offer. It was a beautiful farm and, for the most part, seemed to have been well cared for. The house was small, with a kitchen extending the width of the building. One door opened into a tiny living room, and at the other end of the kitchen, a similar door opened into a dining room. Mae knew right away that the addition promised would have to be built as soon as possible. Three bedrooms and a bathroom comprised the upstairs. The prime requirements of indoor plumbing and electricity were satisfactory.

Avery was delighted with the two large milking barns that had a dairy in between, a large horse barn, and two huge silos. There were two other houses for the hired men and a garage with living quarters overhead if more help was needed. The garage housed a tractor and some other machinery that seemed to be in working order.

Captain McCain made it a point to be on hand after they had looked their fill. After a salary and other stipulations about some changes that needed to be made were agreed upon, it was decided that Avery would be the general manager of Mossback Farm until further notice.

What began as an assumption of two or three years of work turned into almost twenty years. So many things happened during those years that Ella Mae was amazed when one day she looked up as Avery came in for dinner and realized for the first time that he was old. That meant that she must be old, too! How had that happened so quickly?

Her memories traveled back to the war years. Garvin had enlisted in the army almost immediately. Mae was surprised that he passed the physical after going through rheumatic fever.

During the war, their family had special ration coupons for sugar, gasoline, and tires for the car. Butter was rationed also, but that was no problem, as Mae churned their own butter and sold any extra to the people who lived nearby. She also kept a list of regular customers for the eggs her faithful hens supplied every year.

Ben had come home to help on the farm and soon married a lovely girl from North Carolina. Mary Lou graduated from high school and promptly married instead of going to college as they had hoped she would. But it seemed girls at seventeen were very strong willed when it came to love. Before they realized it, Jo was grown up, and she, too, graduated and followed her sister's steps into marriage.

They only had been on the farm a year or so when word came that Captain McCain had been killed in the line of duty. A tearful Mrs. McCain came to tell them the news. She begged Avery to stay on and help her with the farm. She had no idea what the future would hold for her, but for the sake of the boys, she felt she must hold onto the farm.

Mae recalled the many times she looked up from what she was doing to see Mrs. McCain coming for a short visit. There did not seem to be a reason for theses visits, but usually the conversation got around to questions about life after death or how one could know one's prayers were heard.

When Mrs. McCain came on the pretext of needing eggs when she had stopped for eggs two days ago, Mae knew she was coming for more than eggs. It was at these times that she was thankful for the storehouse of Bible verses she had memorized through the years. She was not used to speaking of religious things in ordinary conversation, but she recognized the need for comfort and reassurance in this lady who seemed to have so much and yet so little of the real things of life. It had to be the Holy Spirit who caused Mae to know the right words to say that changed a relationship from employer/employee to friends.

Anytime work was heavy and extra hands had to be hired, Mae had to feed them. This usually was during planting or harvest season, when crops had to be tended at just the right time. It was during the period when almost every able-bodied man was being called into service in the war and farm workers were hard to find that a government official came with the request that Avery take on five German prisoners of war to help on the farm. The official would bring them each morning and pick them up each night. In the meantime, they would be kept busy and thus save the government from having to keep a guard over them; plus it would help with the labor shortage. They were boys who had been raised on a farm, and it would solve two problems at the same time.

The proposal sounded good and should have worked well, but there were problems. Foremost was the language barrier. None of the five could speak English. Also, all of this took place when the fighting with the Germans was at its peak, and these were the people their son was fighting. Avery did not have much patience and had a hard time keeping his voice down when he was trying to show them how he wanted things done.

Ella Mae could not help but see how young they were. These boys should be at home on their father's farm instead of over here among strangers, unable to communicate. It was true some of their people might be trying at this very minute to kill their son, but she doubted if these particular boys understood why all the killing was necessary. She always urged them to eat and wondered what their mothers were thinking. She supposed they might be praying for their sons, just as she did for Garvin. She never forgot the desolate look on their faces when the truck showed up to take them away for the last time.

Her memories moved on to when the war ended and they received a call that Garvin would be arriving at the train station in Aberdeen the next day. Avery took Ben and Mary Lou with him to bring him home. Eileen and her husband came home, and it was a good time. Mae was so overjoyed that he was home and unharmed that she had trouble keeping her attention on what she was doing.

The next days turned into party days. Riley and his family came to visit, and they cooked and ate and talked to their hearts' content. Neighbors and friends from church dropped in to welcome Garvin home and rejoice that the war was finally over and people could get back to life as they always had known it.

But that was not the way it happened. Nothing ever returned back to what it had once been. The job on the farm that was supposed to have lasted for not more than four or five years had lasted for more than twenty. The dream house that was supposed to be waiting for their return was instead sold back to the family from which Avery had bought it. Avery and Mae had become accustomed once again to the work of farm life. Avery had benefited from the monthly income and the perks that came with being in charge of a large operation. This job had provided a sense of accomplishment and a comfortable lifestyle for Mae.

She thought back to an evening some friends from church dropped by. The living room (that Captain McCain had built onto the house as promised) was soon filled to overflowing. This surprise 35th wedding anniversary party was a warm page in her memory book.

Every summer, one or two of the children came home for a visit. Foster was able to visit sometimes, even though he was now the proud owner of the hardware store where he first began his working days. Faye came with her son, David, and one year, she gave birth while there to a beautiful baby girl. Eileen and her husband came frequently. Riley and Anna brought their two young girls in between preaching revivals at neighboring churches.

Garvin eventually had entered the University of Maryland and finished college before entering Temple University near Philadelphia to become a veterinarian, husband, and father, in that order. Ben was tired of the farm by the time the war was over and moved his new wife and daughter back to North Carolina. He sometimes stopped in with the big tractor and trailer he drove around the country for a grocer in West Jefferson. Mary Lou and Jo both lived close enough to come almost every week or so. Their growing families soon filled the dinner table, as their visits often coincided with meal time.

It seemed there was always someone extra at their table, and that was fine. Many tales were told over the long table. Somehow, they never had bothered to eat in the dining room, except on the occasions when the family members filled both rooms. Otherwise, they remained at one end of the kitchen and reminisced until the food was put away and the dishes were finished.

Mae watched Avery in the next few days and wondered why she had not noticed how his steps had slowed. She knew it took her a little longer to get things done around the house, too, but somehow the knowledge of the toll the years were beginning to take had not sunk in. She noticed more and more that they were not as active as they needed to be; therefore, it was not a big surprise when Avery sat down one night after supper and suggested they have a little talk.

"How would you like to have a small farm that would be our own again?" he asked.

"I'm ready when you are," Mae replied. "I've been thinking that it might be time for us to start thinking ahead a little." She did not need to ask Avery if he had prayed about this. Long years of living together had instilled that habit in both of their lives.

So it was that Ella Mae had to begin packing again. This time she had to get new packing boxes, and she noted that it took a few more than she had used before. Stuff had a way of accumulating.

Avery and Mae both had mixed feelings about leaving this farm. It had been a good place for them over the past years. Avery had been able to put aside a little each month, so they would not be leaving empty handed.

Ella Mae did not worry about where she would live next. She knew Avery would see that her two requirements were met: electricity and indoor plumbing. Other than those two, she was ready to relax a little and know that what they put forth from now on would be theirs alone.

Her mind traveled over the places they had lived and the ways God had blessed their family at each turn of the road. Someday they would make their final move, but there was nothing morbid about the thought of going to their heavenly home. She would not have to pack because she would be taking nothing with her except the joy of seeing her Savior and the loved ones who had gone on already. She smiled at the thought of Avery's favorite Scripture verse. It was true. Ella Mae had been young, and now she was old, and she never had seen her children begging for bread.

Epilogue

THE REAL ELLA Mae lived to be 92 years of age. She out lived her husband and three of her eight children.

Ella Mae's pastor summarized her as "the happy lady" who wore a smile that was so real, he knew this was not some superficial happiness, but rather an incredible joy which sprang from the depth of her spirit.

He recalled her sense of humor. To him she was an encourager, an inspiration, a spark, a light in the darkness. One could not stay in her presence and brood. She would not let you. She was too full of life and love and hope and faith. She obviously cared a great deal for others, for no one that full of joy and humor could be self-centered. She built her world around her family and others.

Ella Mae

Ella Mae was a Christian without an apology. She was loyal to her family, her church, and her pastor. She believed that life was a gift from God and to be born again was an even greater gift. Because she believed Jesus, she believed in heaven. She would tell all of you who read these words to look for her when you make that journey. You will know her by her happy face.

WinePressPublishing
Great Books, Defined.

To order additional copies of this book call:
1-877-421-READ (7323)
or please visit our website at
www.WinePressbooks.com

If you enjoyed this quality custom-published book,
drop by our website for more books and information.

www.winepresspublishing.com

"Your partner in custom publishing."

CPSIA information can be obtained at www.ICGtesting.com
Printed in the USA
LVOW041216170512

282162LV00001B/13/P